for Cerena,

you can *do whatever you want to do.......*

THE ORDEAL

Pt 1 "Freeney"

by Clay-Doh the World Destroyer

PROLOGUE

Allenville is a close knit community nestled in the pine valleys of the lower Concordia Mountain range. Home to several species of indigenous trees including the Red Oak, Cottonwood and ever pervasive Lodgepole Pine, Allenville is renowned for it's lush forest, thick vegetation and not least, it's remarkable fog. As the moisture from the coastal regions saunters through the natural avenues and grooves produced by the low altitude mountains, humidity from the forest creates a blanketing mist which clings to the village like a garment of cloth.

Eerie for some maybe, comforting for those who've spent their lives here in this rural American suburb. Using the resilient smog as an excuse to cuddle a little bit longer with their loved ones, the casual nature of the town allowing for workdays to begin as late as 9:30am on particularly obscured days.

In America, Halloween has always invoked a diaspora of emotions. The onset of fall brings the years struggles to a foment as the inner alarm clocks from past generations remind us to make sure the crops are well tended to for the last minute harvest preparations.

Children, industrious with heightened senses in anticipation of the impending candy free for all, are sliding into their respective costumes. This may be their biggest test of the year. The harder they work for the remainder of the evening, the more they can spoil their dinners the following months to come. The more judicious ones can even make their stashes last until Easter sometimes. There's this palpable electricity in the air as mischief grins with excitement at the possibilities the night may bring.

Though the moon had been visible for most of the afternoon as it's golden hue takes shape, so too a pair of sinister eyes awaken and turn their attention to the unsuspecting commune. With reptilian pupils enclosed by amethyst irises focusing, squinting with spite, the consciousness of the beast reveals itself upon the unwitting inhabitants of Allenville, USA. No one notices it and a moment later, the apparition is no longer visible.

CHAPTER 1

"I hate Halloween. Last year, my gramma's house got egged three times and the worst part is, I think it was those same little bastards she gave her peanut brittle to. But you know how kids are these days, if it don't come in a Nestlé wrapper, they won't eat it. But who knows? Maybe their folks made them throw it out anyway. You never can be too careful, ya know? With all these nut jobs puttin razor blades in candy apples every time you turn around. Whuddya gonna do? Sure, you're mammy made you throw away your candy but you live with'em, see'em every day. You're better off takin it out on the house that gave it to you."

Dr. Kovac didn't lift his head from his paperwork.

"Don't you think it's sad the way the corporations cannibalize our holidays? It's always about the candy with the kids. I bet most of em' out there don't even know what a haunted hay ride is. I remember we used to have sumn called a fair. I won third place for my pig when I was 12. Looked forward to it all year. Used to feed mine cornmeal, the others got slop. Used to talk to it too. The whole community came together. Now it's all about trick-or-treat, trick-or-treat. The kids get out of school and by the time they're done, it's 8 o'clock. Dark. Cold. Everyone's tired. My sister said her kids brought home a grocery bag each. And for what? Just a bunch of diabetis' waitin ta happen. For free, too. Typical American value system. You wake up one day and get you a bag and go home to home demanding candy for free and expect to be compensated. And why not? Everybody else is doin it. Why? Nobody asks. I swear, summa these kids don't even say trick-or-treat. They just knock on the door and open up their bag. And don't look for a thank you either. And there's their parents standing on the sidewalk with their arms folded in case you have the audacity to refuse. It's extortion! It's entitlement! It's redistribution of wealth! I'd be willin to bet Willy Wonka is a Goddamn liberal!"

Kovac continued scribbling on his ledger. He had the posture of one taking a final exam, engrossed in the endless record keeping which came with the territory. Every so often, he would pause long enough to change out a piece of paper and seamlessly transition into copying it.

An exception to the rule in this digitized

21st century, Dr. Kovac insists on keeping his own hand written records of all the patients that come into his care at Allenville State Hospital. *Computers make mistakes*, he would say, *I don't.*

The office was furnished with all of the standard issue psychiatry widgets. There was the obtrusive ticking of the cuckoo clock. Some wondered if it had been placed there in poor taste but the more observant were forced to conclude it to be a particularly aggressive accessory. Most likely an attempt to rouse outrage at the sheer inappropriateness of it's presence, given the setting. A good psychologist gets you out of your comfort zone.

There was the obligatory suspended metal orbs no one ever felt compelled to interact with and, to top it all off, there was the forever unquenchable drinking bird, requiring the minimalist of suggestions to resume it's perpetual conquest of a petri dish of water.

Hudgens had finally gotten tired of talking. Even though several moments had passed and no response came from Kovac's desk, he didn't register even the slightest bit of annoyance. He knew all of his remarks had been properly stored in their corresponding bins in Dr. Kovac's head. It might take five minutes, sometimes ten but a perfectly reasonable response would inevitably surface. The ticks of the clock were intermittently dispersed by the occasional water droplet noise from the beak of the insatiable drinking bird.

Mr. Hudgens never questioned in his inner conscience Kovac's elongated response times. He was his employer and a doctor for Christ's sake and he was grateful for an equally superior mind to converse with. One could be driven positively insane listening to the unintelligible gibberish regurgitated by the peons composing the nurse and security staff but as Staff Administrator, it was his unfortunate burden to tolerate this inanity on a daily basis including weekends and double shifts on holidays or when Dr. Kovac was away on business or vacation.

"Are you familiar with the Bod Fly, Mr. Hudgen's?" The question emerging from an unquantifiable nook in the far reaches of the space/time continuum.

"I like to watch Animal Planet sometimes but not Discovery channel. Ever since the crocodile hunter died......"

"A fascinating species." Kovac cut him off. "The female inserts her larva into the brain of an unlucky worker ant. The ant survives the ordeal and lives on until the larva hatches out of it's skull upon maturation."

A small, uncomfortable silence ensued.

"Kinda like that movie 'Alien', huh?"

"Correct, Mr. Hudgens. Kind of like the movie 'Alien'. Likewise, this is the method by which American customs originate and take shape." Dr. Kovac speaks in a punctuated, heavily accented, Eastern European cadence. He ended his phrase with a glance from a pair of icy blue eyes, half concealed by their lids with unamusement.

Hudgens felt compelled to change the subject even though the doctor's diagnosis brought about more questions than it had answered. It made sense but could only be concluded to be unsettling at best, especially given the proximity to dinnertime.

"We only have one more ward left to visit today, doctor. Did you wanna go ahead and knock it out before supper?"

CUCKOO

CUCKOO

The bird emerged from it's nest behind the powder blue doors located just below the face of the clock every quarter of an hour.

Dr. Kovac, who'd returned diligently to his loggings, purportedly responding more to the clock than his assistant's queries, coolly placed his fountain pen on the desk, returned his head from it's 45 degree position.

"Yes, let us."

"Yes, my lord. It pleases me greatly that I might assist thee in the Great Work. But, I do not know the location where Pastor Coleman has hidden The Book."

SCREE

SCREE

"Yes, they are building a basketball gymnasium behind the annex, next to the new parking lot. I remember, I helped clear some of the brush over there."

SCREE

SCREE

"I know not, my liege. The chest had a white tree emblazoned. But there was nothing inside. He must of known I would come for it."

SCREE

SCREE

"Oh, yes, master. Thank you. Though your instruction hath given me so much comfort and warmth already, without you I would have no reason to push onward. I exist only to assist in The Struggle."

SCREE

SCREE

"I am not a greedy man. The Struggle is an end to a means. Material reward could only devalue my sacrifice. My recompense shall lie therein only when the blood of the Believers soaks the ground of this wretched coven of iniquity."

SCREE

SCREE

"Master, if I but had wings like you, I could help you vigorously survey the land. We could follow Coleman. We could uncover The Book."

SCREE

SCREE

"Oh! Oh! Oh, yes! Oh, yes! My king! If it is thy will, I hath great joy partaking in this sacred cause. This is such an exciting time to be alive! This is such a momentous time! It is so exhilarating! It is so wonderful! I once thought I knew what happiness was but I was wrong. Like a savage living amid civilization, not ever knowing what he was missing. I was foolish. I was misguided. But I was ignorant. My lord, you saved me from servitude. You released me from the bondage of my creator. I owe you my life and I give it freely. Money, parties, expensive drugs, women, even the birth of my own children were but mere droplets compared to a raging river now that I have come into the care of your ever watchful eye!"

SCREE

SCREE

CHAPTER 2

"Can Maddy come out and play?"

Bob frowned. *How long did you spend practicing that in front of the mirror?*

"Uh, yeah. Hold on a minute." They were just at the age where he couldn't justify referencing his Remington but old enough to where he wanted to.

When the Henley's front door reopened, there was an adolescent girl standing in his place. Even with the dissipating October sun shining from behind the boys, the grease from their cheeks and forehead bristled.

"Ready yet? I'm not gonna stand by and wait around for these 5th graders to get all the good stuff."

"Yeah, if I get stuck with a bag full of those big orange peanuts, you'll have to pay me back." Patrick always guarded his possessions closely, having come from money. Funny how well to do kids could have so much, yet still own nothing themselves and be aware of that when with their friends.

"Hold on. We have to take Jimmy or I can't go."

The boys looked at each other. Bummer,

dude. Nothing could put the kibosh on a teenager's hopes for exploration of the fairer sex than
the younger brother tag along, an ancient tactic
employed by mindful guardians.

The door closed once again.

"Relax, Rory. You weren't going to get any,
anyway."

"You don't know that!" Rory gushed.

"Even if you did, you'd probably cut your willie to ribbons on her braces."

Rory grimaced at the imagery but couldn't
deny the amusement.

"Only one way to find out!"

They were a mismatched pair of 8th graders.
Neither had made the cut for their naturally
preselected social groupings they should've been
healthily ingrained in by now. Rory, from the
wrong side of the tracks, hadn't been considered
tough enough to roll with the neighborhood
hoodlums. Patrick, certainly well off but never
fully recovered from an odd first impression made
when his family relocated from Cleveland four
years previous.

"A guy like you just doesn't get a girl like her.
She's off limits. You're better off hanging around
in the friend zone and roaching on the crumbs
that fall off her ugly friends' table. Ha ha ha ha!"
Even Patrick had to be pleased with the delivery
of that blow to reality.

Rory didn't register the pain. "Takes one to
know one. Heh, heh."

"What are you guys laughing about?"

Madison's head was peeking out from the

abyss within the household. Wearing a mischievous grin, she couldn't remotely conceal her eavesdropping, their silence a damning indication of guilt.

She finally emerged from the doorway in her signature pink, plastic rimmed glasses. None of them were wearing costumes. They'd hedged their bets and sided with a more pragmatic approach this year. Having recently begun their growth spurts, they might look a little bit desperate in costume. Some people wouldn't notice. Probably. But others might feel inclined to save their candy payouts for the 'real' trick-or-treaters. The one's where you say, 'And what are you supposed to be?' And they don't usually listen to the response, if they wait for it at all. Timid little voices drowned out by the overpowering symphony of candy wrappers dropping from high altitude into the mandatory, plastic Jack-o-lantern in likeness, little pails. 'Trick or....' SPLASH! Couple handfuls of candy. SLAM! 'Get off my lawn'. At least they were appealing to the integrity of the homeowners they were patronizing. *Not trying to get over on anybody here. Just want some candy. Thanks. You know, we're still basically kids. But big. And we could actually damage some property if we felt like it. Good. Cool.*

"Rory wanted me to ask you if you'd give him a kiss."

"Did not!"

She giggled. "Oh, I'll give you a kiss alright. A Hershey one."

Rory transitioned to a pigmentation resembling that of a radish. Patrick, regarding his friend's boyish reaction with slight disbelief from the corner of his eye, resumed.

"You two love birds want to get moving? I wanna get this garbage bag full before eight. The Douglas house has a haunted backyard tonight."

Old man Douglas had taken some orange and purple paints to some standard issue white Christmas lights. There were cobwebs and mist machines and rumors this year of a reanimated corpse, most likely Mr. Douglas himself, that would spring to life from some mist coalesced cranny and jump out on unsuspecting victims.

"Patrick, you bean! How on Earth are you going to carry an entire garbage bag full of candy?"

"I don't know, seems like a good problem to have. But how am I supposed to find out with you guys playing tongue hockey every thirty seconds?" He quipped with a smirk.

Rory looked as if he wanted to reach down Patrick's throat and tear his tonsils right out.

Luckily, Madison's little brother Jimmy extinguished the exchange by squeezing through the front door in a red power ranger outfit. Presumably, already lost was the mask or perhaps it was too uncomfortable, the tiny breathing slot would get sweaty and coagulated as he most likely had been wearing it around the house since school let out. He had his plastic jack-o-lantern candy pail in one hand and his faithful teddy bear in the other. He was seven then.

"Haven't seen one of those in a while." Patrick snickered.

"Guys, do you realize how much extra loot we're going to get with this little guy? We're gonna drain this town dry. Then we can ditch the dweeb at the church. They're having a lock-in over there tonight." Maddy informed.

Rory chimed in, "Old ladies are suckers for little boys in tights!"

"Wouldn't you know? Aah yuck, yuck, yuck, yuck."

Jimmy just stared blankly at the entourage. He didn't speak much. He wasn't slow nor had he seen many hardships early on. Then again, perhaps the budding revelation of what life entails is more than enough for some to consider hardship. He typically wore the expression of a youngling processing a disproportionately high amount of information. Surely there would be some adults to consider him 'challenged'. A keen observer might recognize the brilliance of a young mind that absorbs but doesn't feel obligated to vocalize it's analysis. Some say a sign of early intelligence is the ability to lie. Is this not precisely what some portray by sheer omittance? Every opportunity taken to avoid divulgence of one's thoughts and feelings with mama and papa and teacher deliberately is like a little lie in itself. This is where private, untouchable identities are formed. Identities that can only be uncovered by God Himself or maybe some sort of reverse transgression hypnosis.

"Ready to get the big score with us, lil brother?" Maddy coaxed.

He nodded, the corner of a smile forming.

This was his chance to run with the big kids. He sauntered down the three step porch and proceeded to stumble forward awkwardly.

"Jeez! What the hell was that?" Patrick shouted. He was already moving toward Jimmy. If anyone was capable of catching him before he fell, it was him. "Did you see that? Just–"

Jimmy's candy pail was popping with activity. When he fell, it had rolled in a semicircle but it was still jostling and bouncing long after the momentum from the spill should have subsided. Something was......fluttering. Inside it.

"Is that a bird?"

Jimmy had picked himself up by now and was shrinking away back towards familiarity.

Rory reacted decisively. Corralling, flipped the pail over and held it in place.

SCREE-SCREE

SCREE-SCREE

"Dude, it's....a bat."

"Have you ever seen a bat behave like that before? That is weird." A curious discussion was simmering.

"Well, I know they can get rabies." Rory offered.

"Yeah but they're not blind. And they're not stupid. They don't fly somewhere they don't want to."

"This is a good sign, Jimmy. See? The spirit of Halloween comes to you. I knew he was gonna be good luck."

SCREE-SCREE

SCREE

SCREE

Rory was fascinated by his captive. It was still bouncing off the walls in there, flapping it's wings wildly, making a great bit of noise and it's little chirp/screech incantation.

"Rory, stop. Let it go."

He wasn't paying attention though, entertainment spread across his face. The longer the episode unfolded, the more captivating the candy pail became.

"Rory, please." Maddy insisted.

Her voice finally bringing him back.

"Oh. O.k., yeah."

He flipped the pail right side up and the distress instantly ceased.

The Henley's porch light hadn't been turned on yet but the waning sunset provided little clarity as to what was transpiring inside. No shadows were being projected on the thin layered plastic sides. And still, yet even, not a sound emanated from within. The children were no more than a 5 ft radius from the bucket. No one dared peak inside, though curiosity beckoned.

Rory was brave enough. Or if he wasn't, he simply couldn't resist any further, slowly crept up to the pail. He didn't stand over it and look down into the aperture at the top. No. Gingerly, got down on all fours and crawled forward until he was nearly right above it so that he might peer in and make out what was taking place.

The bat was standing upright, it's wings wrapped around each other like a trench coat, wearing a quizzical expression with it's head cocked to the side as if it was wondering what had taken so long for someone to conduct a welfare check. It chirped lightly.

"He's cute. What's your name, little buddy?"

Rory was charmed. He began to notice the piercing, dark purple eyes. After another moment more, the eyes, to him, felt seemingly like the only thing existing in the world with any real substance.

Is this love? He thought.

SCREEEEEEE

The bat hissed ominously. A cloud of bright green gas materialized in front of Rory's face with a poof. It was thick, lush. Rory breathed it in innocently, quickly began coughing with extreme violence.

"Oh, my God!" Maddy shouted. "Somebody help him!"

He was on his back now. She rushed to his side, as those who witness an accident often do, even if their resourcefulness allows them only to kneel around their fellow comrade, prop his or her head up and plead with them, "Are you o.k.? Are you alright?" When they are clearly not alright.

But Rory was alright.

Aside from a cold sweat that had broken out, he was regaining consciousness rapidly.

"Yeah. Yes. Yes, I'm fine. Here, help me up."

The pail was empty.

"What was that?"

"I don't know."

"Are you o.k.?"

"Yeah. Yes."

"What was that?" More urgently.

"I don't know. A bat, I guess."

"What did it spray you with?"

"It didn't spray me, I don't think. It just shot this green cloud at me. Or it made that green cloud come at me or something. Or, it turned into that green cloud."

"Calm down."

Maddy vanished inside, returned instantly with a glass of water, no ice. He guzzled it.

Patrick, "Where's your dad?"

"I don't know. I think he's taking a nap."

"I think it was some sort of Halloween trick. I think someone is playing a trick on us. I bet there's a camera around here or something. O, cool! We might be on TV!"

"Do you want to come inside for a little bit and lie down, Rory?"

Patrick resisted the impulse to make innuendo (the situation was decidedly comical) but Rory was his friend and he was taking far too long to answer her concerns.

"Rory?"

His eyes were wide, focused on something far away. He was standing up now, staring blankly, pupils dilated, even though there wasn't much light outside, taking shallow breaths rapidly. He was scared shitless. No, he was *petrified* with fear. A moustache of sweat had taken shape and his friends' discomfort was reaching an apex.

"What do we do?" Patrick urged.

The kids were standing around, exchanging nervous glances. Their eyes darted back and forth between each other at a high rate. Jimmy was holding his teddy bear so tightly with both arms, it actually looked painful for both him and the bear.

Maddy was the first to take initiative, "I'm going to wake up papa." She said as she vaulted up the steps.

To the young men, it felt like years she was gone. Patrick had one hand on his friend's shoulder, the other on his forearm, trying to ease his trepidation or at least offer a safe passage back from some distant realm where Rory's mind was held captive. Surely there was the perception that Rory's balance was not static in nature.

Soon enough, Mr. Henley appeared behind Madison, leading an unenthusiastic father who worked no less than sixty hours. *What now? They don't pay me enough for this shit.*

"He's just standing there. He won't move." Patrick explained.

Probably what I should've done a second ago, in my bed.

Big Bob eyed the boy skeptically. *I guess they're never too young to start doing drugs. Gotta getem started early, hey! Probably nothing good like what we had.*

"Wanna come inside, son? Got some sodas in the ice box."

Nothing.

Bob attempted to impede his view with a hand gesture but his focus was resolute. He waved the wand in front of his face exaggeratedly.

Still, no.

Oh, man. I carved a pumpkin and Maddy is old enough to keep an eye on her brother. What do I have to do to get a nap around here?

"Come on in. You can ogle my daughter a little bit better in the light." He hadn't truly intended to say that out loud beyond that of a mutter under his breath but he was halfway hoping the boy had picked it up.

"O.k., what did you guys do to him?" He diverted to the conscious.

"Nothing, dad. I promise."

"Yeah, it was that bat."

"You hit him with a bat?"

"No!" Maddy retorted. "You know, it was the flying kind." The look of alarm in her eyes was not far gone, Bob was still expecting a punch line.

"What. Did it bite him or something? Where is it?"

"I don't know. It's gone. I mean, it didn't bite him, I don't think. It was that green gas the bat sprayed him with."

Bob took a moment to digest this. "What are you talking about?" He looked to the others for help.

"Yes, sir. Mr. Henley. She's right. It's true."

He looked over to Jimmy. *Surely, my seven year old will be the voice of reason.* But the youngster only nodded in agreement with the previous accounts. And he wasn't the type to play pranks.

Now we will be going inside, he thought, *before the neighbors start prying. At least there is beer in there.*

"O.k., let's get him inside. Every one calm

down. We'll talk about it in there. Sound o.k., Rory?" Not that he was expecting a reply.

He and Patrick took either side of the boy, placing one hand on his back, one on his elbow, began gently rotating him, trying to guide him toward the house.

O.k., at least his motor skills were still functional. They slowly, steadily got him inside and laid him down on the couch. Maddy brought a cool, wet hand towel and placed it on his forehead. She put forth a glass of water and cupped it in his hand but astutely realized it would be dropped if she didn't hold it for him. He still wasn't here. Keeping with the troubled look, his eyes, they didn't search the room or show any sign of interest in anything pertaining to the physical realm.

"What's his home phone number? I'm going to call his mom."

"I don't know if it would do much good, sir. He comes from like a broken home. His parents probably don't know where he is and wouldn't notice if he didn't come home tonight according to him. I've never even seen them. I just go over there and knock on his window. He doesn't even have a cell phone." Patrick offered.

Maybe that's what's bothering him. Don't know what kids these days would do without their phones.

"What did you say happened again?" Maybe their story had changed.

"It was this bat." Maddy recalled. "It was in Jimmy's jack-o-lantern. He went to go check it out and it sprayed him with this green gas. That's what did it to him."

Robert was growing impatient. "What are you guys not telling me? I'm not stupid, you know. Are you guys on drugs?"

"No! I swear it!"

"Well, I'm about ready to call an ambulance. Or the cops." He threatened, mostly to gage their reactions. But that didn't increase their panic in any perceptible way. Huh.

He briefly explored the ramifications in his mind. If his folks were really some dead beats, would they try to ambulance chase him for medical bills, pain and suffering, gross negligence? They were in *his* living room. In *his* house. Bob didn't much care for that scenario. But should he call 9-1-1? If he didn't have a headache already, when the cops did get there he surely would.

He rolled his mental sleeves up, went over to the boy, shook him thoughtfully.

"Hey, Rory. Are you in there? Hellooo. Anybody there? C'mon back. C'mon back to us. You know you want to. C'mon."

Rory may as well have been a mannequin.

"Hey!" He clapped several times, inches from the boy's face but to no avail.

"Dad, stop." His daughter's voice seeped in.

Great. This little punk is trying to sniff my daughter's panties and he's already motionless on my couch. That was quick.

Bob was running out of ideas. Then the wheel barrel in the backyard sprang into his thought process. There. Problem solved. One drugged out teenager on somebody else's porch.

But it's just not an ideal world. Time to man up. He reached for the phone.

That's when Rory, to the relief of the room, finally stirred.

"Uuuuuuuunhhhh." He groaned.

"Rory! Are you alright, sweetie? Are you o.k.?" A concerned Madison inquired. "Here, drink some water." She guided the glass into his hand and towards his mouth. Halfway sat up and reluctantly complied with her directions.

"What happened? Where am I?"

"Bro, you were outta there." Levity was attempting to regroup.

Rory exhaled, placed the glass down, started rubbing his eyes.

"You o.k., son? What happened? Do you remember?"

"No. I mean, I was going to look in that jack-o-lantern and then….." He trailed off with a far away look in his eye. "They're going to kill us all."

Robert Henley grimaced, "Excuse me?"

"They're going to kill us all. Every last one of us." Delivered void of emotion.

"Who's they?"

"I don't know. But they work for the devil."

"They work for the devil?"

"Yes. I saw it. The sky was turned blood red. The town. Everyone. Everything. Was drenched in blood. It was lamb's blood. And everyone's blood. And they were laughing and celebrating."

Man. They don't make 'em like they used to. He'd witnessed a few bad trips in his day but this was a whole different animal.

"Who was?"

"Some people I've seen before. Others, I don't know. They look weird."

You don't say? Well, so much for 'kids say the darndest things'! Gee, if Madison wants to take this guy to the prom one day, I don't know what I'll do.

"Man. Whew!" Rory shook his head as if someone had told a bad joke. Rubbed his eyes with his fingers, aerated his eyelids. "Do you have any food? I'm really hungry."

CHAPTER 3

Ward E11 was Mr. Hudgens' favorite. Not because he particularly liked it but because he liked to be reminded of things. As Dr. Kovac's administrative enforcer, he expected to be reminded a lot. If someone wasn't reminding him of something, he would assume that he should be the one doing the reminding. Dr. Pedrag Kovac didn't like to be reachable, so he relied on Mr. Hudgens as his go-between. He would collect information and redistribute it at his boss' behest. However, state law still required that the resident psychiatrist make himself available on the unit at least once a week and Dr. Kovac religiously met that requirement but was meticulously careful not to exceed it. Overzealous hands on psychoanalysis by the provider leads to somatic behaviors. If somebody was always holding the patient's hand and babying them, they might start second guessing themselves subconsciously. Critical thinking the unspoken law of the day, *if we want to enable our wards and not become a crutch to their development,* best to leave the conjecturing to the professionals.

The central variable that reminded Mr. Hudgens he was in E11 was the smell. Desperation. Anxiety. Urgency. Failure. Not to mention the undeniable presence of urine and urine. E11 was home to some of A.S.H.'s most paranoid, unstable individuals. Extreme cases of schizophrenia and obsessive compulsive disorder were the norm here. Everyone in this unit had been committed for long term stays. Because of the need for constant monitoring, closed circuit cameras were mounted above every cell. Sometimes Mr. Hudgens wondered if this was truly conducive to recovery for someone with such fragile a grasp on reality. Regardless, he reasoned, if they could take care of themselves, they wouldn't require someone else to do it for them.

"Hi, Dr. Kovac. Hello, Mr. Hudgens."

They willfully sidestepped the safety officer's greeting as they traveled through the door he was holding open for them next to the security kiosk. They kept a brisk pace. The quack wanted to avoid any unnecessary engagement with the patients. One might consider how helpful the doctor's presence really was to the tranquility of the unit. Their concerns were usually unable to be accommodated anyway, if not outlandish in nature to begin with.

Kovac liked to take a furtive peek in on some of the cells at the end of the run. They were reserved for those deemed to be more or less unpredictable. Commonly, by the time they'd reached this point in their treatment, they'd been approved for more than normal dosages of medication and were usually relatively sedated. He liked to make sure the tranquilizers were having the proper effect. Some patients had demonstrated resistance to certain brands. Everyone's body is different.

The doctor of Eastern European descent crept most surreptitiously in his corduroy moccasins, hands clasped behind his back. Resembling a count maybe, he was virtually silent as he approached cell 15. He would gauge the angle of his approach just right in order to have a look in on his stead without them knowing he was ever there. He preferred to assess from a distance based off objective reports and data, his presence among the disturbed only seemed to further their consternation.

Today was a little bit different he noticed. No one appeared to be inside. The room was stoically uniform and devoid of stimulus. Partly for the desired effect of noninterference in the self-reflection and recovery process but also, and perhaps more importantly, virtually any object could be used to inflict pain and damage or even death in the form of a choking hazard or make shift bludgeoning object. Hence, there was little more than a pallet, heavy blanket and commode. So it was rather unmistakable for one to assess that no one was inside the quarters.

"Hudgens, what of Mr. Simon?"

"Same old kook last I heard. Helluva tolerance. Talks to himself constantly."

"Praytell, Mr. Hudgens, why is he not located in his housing?"

Hudgens leaned over to peer through the window slit of the steel reinforced door.

"Mr. Simon is not to be permitted outside of his quarters at this time. There is no one documented on his visitor's list. Why is the patient not in his housing? He is dangerous."

Hudgens leveled an accusatory glare back down the hallway towards the kiosk and beckoned over the guardsman.

"Maybe they're in the middle of moving him to a different unit or something."

Kovac's silent agitation simmered as the safety officer made his way up the corridor. As soon as he was within earshot, Hudgens met him with the question.

"Gregory, where is Mr. Simon? Gary Simon, cell 15."

Gregory changed his expression to a pensive one.

"Excuse me."

He gently ushered himself to the observation window, just to verify for himself. They were telling the truth, though, even a simpleton could determine that. No chance at a tasteless joke. Same disheveled room. Messed up bedding. Grunge. Filth. No Gary. He looked back at Hudgens. This did not look good. Either way he answered, he was going to get his ass chewed at the end of the day. Action. That was the only way to save him now, with the boss man glaring at him as though he had perpetrated the Holocaust or something. Frankly, he could give a damn if one of these retards got free, touched a pizza, maybe even got a piece of ass. They didn't pay him enough to. But he did care about that paycheck. He sidestepped the lingering discomfort by simply activating his walkie-talkie.

BLEEP-EEP

"Control, this is Blakely. Are there any open transfers in E11?" Maybe not best to broadcast a potential missing patient on an open channel.

"This is control. Negative. All cells are occupied."

BLEEP-EEP

BLEEP-EEP

"Can you switch to channel 3 for me?"

"O.K."

This was not good. But the one saving grace was the progression of modern technology, every square foot in the facility was under continuous video surveillance. All the doors were monitored by computer and outfitted to trigger alarms, should they be perforated, along with security personnel issue RFID chip badges. The walkways and perimeters were patrolled hourly. It was a maximum security wing. Of course, his training and Murphy's law had informed him that if a mistake could potentially be made, eventually it would. At the very least, if somebody had gotten out of their cell somehow, surely they couldn't have gotten far. And there *would* be video evidence.

Gregory felt a rush of adrenaline. He had never gotten the opportunity to chase down an escapee before. But, given that he hadn't seen too much action since the conclusion of his football days, he was secretly relishing the chance. Deep down, he knew it wasn't a fair contest, though. He lifted weights, ate well and maintained high morale. Not to mention, a naturally gifted athlete, whoever he would be pursuing would be weak and atrophied from the nutrient deficient food, vitamin depleting medication and lack of physical activity.

"This is control. Can you hear me?" BLEEP-EEP

BLEEP-EEP "10-4. Can you tell me about Mr. Gary Simon in cell #15, Echo 11? He isn't in his room. The doctor is here, wants to see him."

"Standby." BLEEP-EEP

Greg exhaled. Response shouldn't be long. In the meantime, there were two sets of eyes trying to bore holes into him. He avoided eye contact, trying to maintain a portrayal of equal aggravation at some underling's communication failure.

"Mr. Simon cannot be accounted for at this time. Greg, I need you to go in the cell and make sure he's not in there." BLEEP-EEP

It's bad enough we lost track of Charles Manson. Are you really going to make me search a cell for a full grown man in which one cannot possibly hide?

Mr. Hudgens looked as though he was about to snap his clipboard in half over his knee. Without saying anything, he rushed off towards the security kiosk.

Dr. Kovac arched an eyebrow in annoyance and waited patiently behind Gregory. The safety officer quickly located the corresponding key on his pocket chain and inserted it into the lock. *I know no one's in there. Then again, it would be just my luck. That freak is probably perched above the doorway like Spiderman, camouflaged against the off white paint, waiting for me to just waltz right into his trap like a dumb ass.*

He twisted the key, waited for the metallic whir of the bolt lock deactivating and swung the door open. Just for good measure, before he set foot in the living quarters, he poked his head in through the doorway and took a sneak peek up at the ceiling.

Man, this place is really getting to me.

CHAPTER 4

"It's good to see you too, Larry. We're just going to watch a few movies, play some capture the flag and eat pizza until the sun comes up. Oh, and maybe a little Bible study discussion sprinkled in there." Pastor Coleman winked.

"O.K., we'll be back here in a couple of hours then." Larry sat himself in the red Kia Rio with the two children strapped in the back seat. It had been running while the grownups talked.

"O.K., bub-bye."

The senior pastor turned his attention to the click clack of the heels approaching him in the parking lot. It was his wife, Challista.

"Did you order the pizzas yet, honey? We're running out of time and I still have to put the cupcakes in."

She was always a hot mess, maybe that's why he liked her.

"Calm down, sweet heart. It's not the bridge of the USS Enterprise. Just a little sleep over for our parishioner's kids."

"Oh, Barry." She poo pooed his light jab. "I just wanted everything to be ready by the time they get here. I just want everything to be in order."

She had always been high strung but this was uncalled for. Why was she so nervous?

"Are you O.K.? Do you want to talk about something?"

He could see her hands shaking. Her sapphire blue eyes quivered with anxiety. She wore the look of a cocker spaniel, exhausted from a day of gnawing on it's master's slippers.

"Oh, no. I'm fine, dear. Let me have the car keys. I want to grab my glasses."

Barry obliged.

She unlocked the door of their Buick Skylark and started rummaging through her purse. Coleman noted how attractive women never seem to be aware of their display as she bent over, searching through her belongings, her well sculpted rump bobbing in the air. They were an older couple now but she was one of those time-less beauties. Especially with her candy apple red heels and floral design yoga pants, her white lace panties peaking about the waist line. She had al-ways been arm candy status but today was par-ticularly risqué fashion-wise, even for her.

"O.K." Finally had her things, she brought herself back around directly into his arms.

"What's wrong, honey? You're all over the place."

"Whew!" She exhaled pure stress. "It's just something with my sister. She can be so stub-born."

"Tabitha?"

Pastor Coleman released her. She put a hand on his arm.

"It's o.k. I'll talk to you about it later. I'm going to order the pizzas, then I'll call her. I'll be in the kitchen."

Female issues. That figures.

They had built a church together, gone through rather unremarkable baby boomer style lives after meeting in 10th grade and becoming high school sweethearts.

Barry watched as she scurried off towards the multi-purpose area of the church.

"O.K., I'll get the gym set up." He called out after her.

Challista brought herself through the door of the activity center and made a trying effort to steady herself so she could mete out the batter into the muffin trays for the cupcakes. But there was entirely no point. The flood gates were open. The cookie was crumbling to pieces. The oven had been preset, was turned on and, much like Challista Coleman herself, smoldering for hours.

She just hadn't gotten around to her baking that afternoon. She was far too distracted. She didn't know why. But she just knew. But she couldn't deny the bestial urges consuming her. Her body was radiating with heat like a furnace, as a droplet of anticipation and desire trickled from behind her ear, down her delicate neck, across the flesh of her open neck blouse and disappearing into her ample cleavage.

An unexplainable sexual intensity she had never before experienced had descended upon her that afternoon. She became aware of a presence. A dark, insidious presence conquered her mind. There was never any fear. But she knew that there should be. But she couldn't resist. The beast was so powerful, yet so gentle. And her curiosity had delivered her into it's claws.

As she leaned over the counter massaging her neck, it was quite undeniable now. It was approaching. Closer. Closer, still. Closer....... now she felt someone's eyes on her.

"Hello, Challista."

She twirled around, startled, her eyes wide with astonishment as she braced herself against the countertop. She was totally caught off guard, not expecting anyone to walk in on her. She'd gotten lost in her private moment.

It was a hooded man in all black on the opposite side of the kitchen. He raised his nose and sniffed at the air deeply.

"Why, Challista, has your little kitten been running like a tap, you naughty little minx. Your panties are thoroughly soaked, aren't they?"

She was filled with terror. Is this a robbery? He was certainly not supposed to be here. And....her vocal chords would simply not allow her to scream. She wasn't in control anymore. Her body didn't belong to her. She knew she didn't agree with what was happening but she just didn't have the willpower to stop it. Her hormones were in charge right now and, as he slowly stepped toward her, she felt herself submitting to an indescribable degree of indulgence.

She lifted herself onto the countertop and

spread her legs open wide so her hand could cup the moist fabric where her camel toe lay pulsing. Emitting an animalistic groan of satisfaction instantly upon making contact with her clitoris through the nylon, she began vigorously rubbing her lips. She was coming uncontrollably.

She naturally leaned further back and lay on the countertop, her legs spread apart in the air. She alternated between rubbing concentric circles on her most erogenous zones using the three middle fingers of her hand pressed together and slapping herself gently, then progressively harder until her body would convulse with each strike. She could feel her vaginal muscles flexing violently in climax and a broad range of musical notes flowed freely and unpredictably from the chamber of her mouth.

Gary Simon finally approached her and firmly grabbed her feet, pushing them back behind her head so her legs formed the shape of parentheses. Her hands instinctively obliged and took their position on the back of her knees to hold them in place. She was about to get fucked.

The ravenous intruder, still hooded in his black Russell sweatshirt, promptly grabbed her tights by the waist band and tore a chasm down the middle of her pelvis. Her panties were next. He shredded them to pieces in the same manner.

She could no longer contain herself. She meowed enthusiastically, "Ooooooh! Oh yes, master! Oh yes, my love! Yes, my lord! Yes! Come into me! Please! Please! Please!!!" She was panting and breathing deeply, her body twitching with anticipation.

The hooded madman grabbed her hair with one hand firmly, tilting her head to the side. His other hand, brought together his index and middle finger forming a 'gun' symbol. The fingers fused together by some nefarious process, formed a phallus which proceeded to elongate to an equine length.

Gary's purple eyes glared with determination. He made sure she was locked into his gaze as he eased the phallic object formed from his fingers into her narrow vaginal cavity, she, shrieking with delight and surprise at every increment of penetration. Once he felt he had reached the furthermost depths of her cervix, he continued to proceed as she began to stretch more and more than she thought possible. All of the air in her lungs exited. She was inundated, her eyes bulging with shock.

"Where is the book with the white tree on the cover?" Gary interrogated.

"What?" She squeaked, caught off guard by the deflection, still focusing on the pain/pleasure of the moment.

"The leather bound, ancient book with the white tree symbol on it. Where is it? I demand to know."

"My liege, I don't know what you're talking about."

"You filthy cur! How dare you deny me the truth."

With that he began pumping her aggressively.

"Oh, my God! Oh, my God! You bastard!" She
yelled. It was half ecstasy, half outrage.

"You petulant bitch!" He responded. "I am
an ambassador for the king of this realm! I am the
ultimate authority in this room! You will answer
truthfully! You will obey to my satisfaction! It is
of your volition that you do so!"

He released the fistful of her locks, gave her
two jarring smacks.

"Oh! Oh, yes! God! OK. Yes! I'll tell you! I
promise I will! Whatever you want!"

He was attacking her birth canal so seriously now that she could feel her cervix ripping.
He was quite literally trying to rupture her intes-
tinal lining. She began gurgling and having difficulty speaking.

"Ah! You're hurting me! I swear I don't know
anything about a book. I swear it!" She shouted.

"You're lying. If you keep lying to me, I'll
kill you. Now tell me! Tell me!!!"

"What is going on in here?" Pastor Coleman
had heard the commotion and screams of distress
and was now attempting to decipher the spectacle before him.

His wife of thirty six years was lying on the
kitchen countertop, twisted into a pretzel, yell-
ing obscenities and apparently engaging, shame-
lessly, in some kind of extreme form of masturbation.

You think you know a person
She instantly snapped back to reality.

"Barry, I..." Trailing off at the realization
of her vastly inappropriate appearance she must

surely be portraying. "Oh, my God. What have I been doing?"

CHAPTER 5

"How's that?"

Rory looked up from his plate and gave a wide grin. A full glass of milk and an assortment of cold cuts, cheeses and breads sat before him. Also pickles, mayonnaise, mustard and even ketchup. Some kids put it on everything.

Bob regarded him with an arched eye brow and deliberately watched to make sure the vittles were making their way down his throat. He watched for his gullet to move like a mother revels in her own child's completion of the gestation process. Given what had unfolded in his living room moments before, he was treating the normally routine procedure like an undetonated pipe bomb.

The kids were all sitting at the table. Everyone was watching Rory. If someone could eat a plate of corned beef, they must be ok. Jimmy was holding his teddy by the arm and had reverted to sucking his thumb. He'd been weaned off of the nervous habit since he was five but the stress of the night had caused everyone to cope differently. *Seem to remember reaching for a cigarette at this point in the past.* Of course, once the kids came around, Linda had banned them from the house.

He'd stopped sneaking smoke breaks about eighteen months after Madison was born.

Oh, my God. Linda!

She would be getting home from work soon.
Sure, everything was under control but 15 years
of marriage had taught Bob to pick his battles
and not make any unnecessary scenes within the
household, which was indisputably her nest. As
long as Bob could manage a scotch and maybe a
decent nap, he didn't give a damn what anybody
else did. It wasn't that he didn't care. Quite the
opposite. He just didn't want anyone to interfere
with his happiness. And as a self-professed problem solver, he felt obligated to embark on a fix
it mission for those he was given to care for. So,
to avoid hypocrisy, he was forced to do the same.
He viewed this philosophy as patently American.
Just don't interfere with anyone's life, liberty and
pursuit of happiness. Why was that not plainly
obvious to everyone else?*One helluva Halloween so
far......for the kids.*

"Anybody want a popsicle?" *Let's just try to
ease on out of this quagmire*, he thought. He was
met with little resistance. "Madison, want to help
me get some out of the freezer in the garage? Chocolate for you, right Jimmy?"

Jimmy smiled and offered a nod of affirmation.

She met him in the garage. "What are we
going to do, daddy?"

"Actually, I was kind of hoping you could
tell me." He grimaced. "He's your weird friend."

"He's not weird. And aren't you supposed to

be the adult?"

Mr. Henley considered this. She had a point.

"Well, does he not act like this sometimes? I mean, does he have, you know, problems?"

"Actually, no. He's pretty well balanced. I guess his mom and dad don't really give a care."

"Yeah but how am I supposed to explain this to your mother? Yeah, the boy got entangled with an enchanted bat. You know, normal teenager stuff." Grabbed a couple of fudge sickle two-packs, one for each hand.

Maddy giggled. "Yeah. Huh, huh. I don't know. Dad, that really happened."

"I believe you, sweetheart."

But he really didn't. Moreover, Robert Henley hadn't the slightest semblance as to what had actually occurred between the kids. Were they playing some morbid prank? Did they really experience something? Or did they simply misconstrue a perfectly explainable event in their unformed minds, making it wholly outlandish and ultimately falling for their own bullshit? He didn't know and he was beginning to not care. Fast. That fat boy was in there chowing down like a starving caterpillar and it's Halloween. *Way to go. You got me.* At least the other one seemed to have his head on straight. Yes, these kids were going to trick-or-treat and Bob was going to have some well-earned alone time with Mrs. Henley. He'd share an inside joke with his daughter at the breakfast table in the morning. Hmm, better than a Tim Allen movie.

"OK, I got ice cream! Who wants some?"

Hopefully no trick-or-treaters would ring the

doorbell right now or he might be forced to give them popsicles too. He didn't even have a candy dish prepared and he was probably going to hear about it from Linda. Hadn't he done a poor enough job selecting candy in the past to be excused from doing it again? She would probably bring some anyway. Besides, he had a different kind of candy for her.

The kids gobbled them up without hesitation. He knew they most likely could use a warm meal but this was a night created for spoiling dinners.

"Feeling better, big guy?" He prodded Rory.

"Oh yes, Mr. Henley. Thank you very much. I've never had corned beef before. I liked it."

"OK. Well, it's getting late. Are you guys still going to get candy tonight? You know she has to be back by 9:15."

"Uh, yeah. I'm ready when you guys are." Patrick spoke up first.

I don't think he was expecting me to say that. See? I knew I could be 'the cool dad'.

CHAPTER 6

Patrick and Madison exchanged nervous glances as they left the house. *He really doesn't believe us, does he? Hmm, nope. If he did, he wouldn't have let us leave.* Now it had gotten to the point where they were beginning to question themselves. Rory was fine, making small talk and seemingly oblivious to what had just taken place. Jimmy appeared to have moved on as well and could be seen bouncing along the sidewalk like an armed spring ready to release upon whatever house the big kids might suggest. They knew what they had seen was real but if Rory wasn't talking about it, they didn't want to bring it up. Not only because it was uncomfortable to think about but they also didn't want to risk reawakening any latent, volatile thing residing in their friend.

However, it was really bothering them. Maddy turned to Patrick, "What are we supposed to do?"

Staring at the ground, avoiding eye contact, "I don't know."

"Patrick, I know what I saw."

"Me, too. We all saw, even Jimmy."

"I can't believe my dad didn't do anything."

"Yeah, he really didn't believe us. Did he?"

"No."

By now, Jimmy had hit on a few two-story homes and was safely distracted with some fun size Milky Ways he was sharing with Rory.

"I don't know what to do." She lamented.

"There is one thing." Without waiting for a reply, "Alma."

"Who is that?"

"The Mexican lady, down by the park. She knows things."

"This is crazy."

"One time, my cousin, she went on a date with this guy. He had a weird family. She didn't really like him and he didn't get a second date. But he got mad. He started calling her and showing up places she would go after school. This went on for about two weeks then she got sick. Real sick. And she started speaking in tongues and throwing up and stuff. It was like *The Exorcist.* They were going to take her to the hospital but they couldn't get her to cooperate with them. Then, Ms. Alma showed up and cured her. She had some mixtures and herbs and stuff. She said that boy had cursed her and he was evil. Her parents had some camera put up and one night they caught him placing a small statue of a devil with a long nose on their front doorstep while they were asleep."

"Wow!"

"Let me get some of those Lemonheads. Yeah. It got so bad, her dad eventually baited him into the house and held him down until the cops got there."

"Jeez." Maddy allowed the allegory to sink

in for a moment. "Well, I guess we should go there. What else can we do?"

"I don't think you truly appreciate the gravity of the situation, Detective Rosicky."

Martin was staying awake. He really was. He was standing with his hand in his pocket, straining crappy coffee through his bushy moustache out of a small Styrofoam cup, listening to Dr. Kovac lecture him. Amazing how people act like they're extending state of the art hospitality when they wheel out a generic cup of Joe, delivered by Sysco, out of an ancient coffee maker and throw some non-dairy creamer into the concoction like they're powdering a baby's diaper. No. He was a cop. He knew what coffee was supposed to taste like. Personally, would never offer it without an accompanying pastry. He didn't care how stereotypical it was. In his mind, it was one of the main perks of protecting the populous.

"Mr. Simon is an unusual case. His body seems to take no effect from the medication we prescribe and I can assure you we have ordered the maximum dosages allowable by the state. He hasn't slept in two weeks. He is physically fit and athletic. He displays a remarkable disdain for society."

"OK, so who dropped the ball? How did this happen? What's really going on here?"

Dr. Pedrag Kovac swept a piece of lint from the collar of his woolen jacket. With his trimmed beard and vest, tie and even pocket watch, he was no stretch for the Freud role. Rosicky half expected him to produce a wooden pipe and stoke the tobacco from the flame of a match. Was everything at this hospital cliché? *Wait till you see the office*, a staff member could've said.

"In the interest of transparency, I'm not completely sure. The unit is under twenty four hour video surveillance. The playback has revealed nothing. The patient can be seen entering his cell after being escorted back from the showers. The computer log recorded that his door was properly secured and it was checked hourly since that time elapsed. His door was subsequently not opened between then and now and there is absolutely no chance of escape from inside the secure room. I suspect some kind of assistance from an individual amongst our staff but still, questions remain. If someone had deemed fit to escort a decoy patient to Simon's cell, where then is the afore mentioned decoy?"

"Sounds like a good ol fashioned cluster fuck."

He could tell the foreign born doctor was unfamiliar with the euphemism, though his demeanor betrayed no evidence of discontent. Detective Rosicky turned his attention to the manila folder containing Gary Simon's information. Thirty six years old. 5'11", 176 lbs. Black hair, brown eyes. There was the standard issue scar under his left eye, seemingly from a knife wound. No tattoos. No Children. Never married. No known family members still living. His profile picture carried a gaze of focused anger coupled with a well-worn, disgruntled frown. Who was

Gary Simon? How had he found his way to this cesspit of madness he'd somehow managed to escape? Hmmm. Aggravated assault with a deadly weapon. Had been declared 'not guilty by reason of insanity' and the subsequent spiral of confusion had cost him the last five years of his unenviable life. Four institutions later, here he was. In a cage with a bunch of others deemed to be too dangerous for society, though technically none of them were facing criminal charges. People tend to forget these people even exist as they usually are subjected to a smorgasbord of psychotropic medications until there aren't enough brain cells in their Swiss cheese like noggins to further justify their existence in a maximum security unit and they are shipped off to a regular care mental health facility or group home where they live out their days in front of the unbiased glow of the television amid an unending deluge of processed meals and state certified supervision. According to the file, Gary tended to have long, drawn out conversations with himself. Whenever they'd entered his room to clean it, a number of symbols were discovered to have been carved into various places under the bed and desk.

Rosicky closed the file and handed an empty Styrofoam cup to a scrupulous Mr. Hudgens.

"I'm going to put out an A.P.B. for this man. In the meantime, keep the cell exactly how it was at the time of absconding. I'm going to send somebody over here to analyze how he might've escaped and collect some evidence."

CHAPTER 7

Challista hopped down from the counter and looked for something to cover herself with, settled on her hands. Crouching in an awkward position, she was essentially bare from the waist down. Her horror was truly reality now. Like one of those ultra-humiliating dreams in which one becomes aware that they are exposed before an audience of their peers, to embarrass herself in front of the one person she respected most was especially devastating. *My God*, what was he thinking about her right now? How was he going to handle this? The pastor's wife just doesn't do things like that. What about the church? If word of this got out, it could ruin them financially. Would he even be able to tolerate being seen in public with her? Everyone knows how news travels in small towns.

Coleman's eyes were bulging with fury. It looked like he wanted to say, or shout, a lot more but he may have been too angry to speak even. He hadn't truly been this upset in twenty five years, when they'd had their first miscarriage. And even then, he hadn't directed any of his rage toward her. He knew it wasn't her fault.

Now his fists were balled. Actually, she

couldn't remember seeing him this angry before at any time. Ever. He had gotten in a couple of fist fights in high school, though she hadn't actually witnessed them herself. When they settled down, he'd developed into more of the strong, silent type. Then, of course, once he'd discovered his faith, his affect became even more serene. The comfort and contentedness of someone who feels no sense of uncertainty, it is profoundly tranquilizing. Thus, he was just the type of guy no one gave a hard time. Not that there was the perception that he would do anything if someone did, per say. People simply did not view him as a threat.

Now Barry came over to her, his face was all scrunched up in disbelief. He mechanically took off his jacket and stooped down to cover her up. She was sobbing hysterically. He wanted to say something, sound off with a bevy of questions but she was clearly too distraught to expect any cogent reply. *Could my wife be having some kind of midlife crisis? Is she having a psychotic break? What kind of person, let alone the wife of a congregation's shepherd, juxtaposes herself on the kitchen counter, the same counter the children's cupcakes are prepared on for Christ sakes, and begins masturbating like a Goddam animal or something?*

Barry kept replaying the images seared into his mind's eye when he had first happened upon her in the activity hall area, trying to make sense of it all. But it just didn't add up. The more he analyzed the situation, he began to realize how strange it really was. He'd instinctively followed the shrieks and screams he'd heard reverberating down the hallway to discover a familiarity in the woman's voice to his dismay, reality dawning on him with every fateful step as he clung desperately to the futile comfort of denial. Maybe he was just imagining things. No. Maybe it was some other woman. Perhaps some other clergy member or congregation couple had succumbed to their lusts when they thought no one was around. Maybe some high school kids or party people, exploring their most baseless and tawdry whims. Who knows? Maybe even a couple of transients, intoxicated on a cocktail of assorted street drugs had settled on the church as a love nest no one would suspect them to be on a Thursday night. No. It was Challista. But who could she be with? Who would betray him so brazenly? In his own church. With her husband so reprehensibly close by. He'd never elicited those kinds of primal outcries from her before during their bedroom escapades. Could she be fulfilling a level of carnal pleasures he could never have hoped to provide her? As he crept closer, his grief turned to concern as the satisfaction in her intonations transitioned into agony.

Forcing himself to confront his fears, his anger changed to confusion when he finally turned the corner and let his eyes fall upon his dear wife locked in a passionate tryst, only her assailant was nowhere to be seen. Her body continued to flex and gyrate in a seemingly bestial type of convulsion however, she was very much alone and her hands were nowhere near her private regions. Further adding to the puzzlement, there could be no denying she was clearly being violated, only by some kind of invisible object. Her labias splayed unnaturally wide, collapsing and exploding in simulation of physique altering intercourse. What kind of bedevilment was this? Yes. She was clearly engaged in coitus but no one else was in the room.

Coleman wore a wounded expression. His untrusting eyes darted around the room as he tried to console her.

"Who was it? Where is he?" He demanded.

Was she cheating or was he looking for a rapist? It didn't matter now. The normally docile Coleman was on vacation.

He reached for his cell phone, started to dial 911 then thought better of it. With all these children and parishioners set to arrive within the hour, if he was going to fill the parking lot with blue and red flashing lights, he'd better be sure about it.

"OK, Challista. I'm going to need you to tell me something. What was happening here?"

She was still pouring water, her make up a sticky mess. "Oh, Barry. I'm so sorry. I'm so sorry. I don't know what happened."

"Are you sure? This doesn't make any sense. Look, I'm your husband of thirty years. I deserve the truth. Are you seeing someone?"

"No! No, I swear I'm not."

"Then what the hell was happening? Was someone attacking you?"

"No! I don't know!"

She brought her head up from her hands and gazed into his eyes, searching for mercy. She was very convincing in her desperate plea for salvation.

Something caught his eye as she crouched. At first, amidst the chaos, his mind had subconsciously grouped together some of the items in the room and thought it was most likely some chocolate cake batter that had possibly spilt onto the Formica surface. But now he could see: she was dripping into a pool of blood.

"Oh, Lord! You're bleeding!"

He'd been surreptitiously hoping there could be some way, some chance, they could maybe sweep this whole thing under the rug, just for the time being at least, and put a happy face on for the lock-in until the kids had finally gone home in the morning but now her livelihood was at stake. Lord! Had she truly been impaled so violently as to have caused massive hemorrhaging? Barry winced with pain at the suggestion. Surely, there was far more to this than he could be expected to comprehend and it was all too much. The children would have to wait.

"Come on. Let's go to the hospital."

CHAPTER 8

By now the foursome had made their way down two whole avenues and reached the park separating the two neighborhoods. It was a fairly large park containing a formidable duck pond and sprawling thicket, replete with hike and bike trail. Their route would require them to traverse a noteworthy meadow through which a foot path had been worn. In recent times, the neighborhood association had succumbed to pedestrian traffic and allowed gravel to be laid down. The barrier between middle and lower class had always been inconvenient at best by car, despite the proximity, due to the odd layout of the city. Now, those on foot and bicycle could travel back and forth within a roughly ten minute interval.

In spite of the usual degree of humidity cultivating Allenville's infamous mist, the wind had allowed for a mostly visible night. The stars were out in full force and a waxing gibbous moon shown big and bright in the crisp Autumn sky.

Jimmy was beaming with pride at his production and would pause every so often to shuffle through his bag of assorted sweets and empty wrappers (Maddy wouldn't allow him to discard them on the ground). Once they had reached the midway point near the duck pond, Rory produced a cigarette and a lighter from the inside pocket of his jacket.

"Wanna smoke a square?" He addressed the group.

"Where did you get that?" Madison scowled.

"From my dad, when he wasn't looking."

No one jumped at the opportunity but they didn't offer any protests either to their friend lighting up. They knew it was gross but it was cool too. Had to be eighteen to get one so they still owed some semblance of respect to the one who could make such an acquisition.

They formed a semicircle around their friend as he wrestled with the cheap corner store lighter. Probably brand new, still full with butane but too shoddily constructed to offer workability to a fourteen year old trying to spark it, into the wind at that. He flicked it repeatedly without success.

"Here, let me see it. Cup your hands." Patrick snatched it from his grasps and began struggling with it himself. *Hmm, 'made in Thailand". Come a long way just to misfire.*

"Turn this away. Your facing right into the wind, dumbass."

Rory adjusted until the wind was at his back as Patrick hobbled around him to resume his position. This time he flicked it on with the first try, illuminating Rory's face.

"There. Got it."

Rory dragged on the stogie and predictably coughed out the smoke, extinguishing the flame. As he struggled to regain his breath, his face red, their attention was averted to the night sky for a hideous screech had pierced the air, ducking everyone's head down and raising their shoulders with discomfort.

SCREEEEEEE

SCREEEEEEE

They turned their attention to the direction the sound had emanated, towards the moon. It had the characteristics of an eagle or hawk, some kind of bird of prey, a raptor to say the least. Even more like the velociraptor depicted in *Jurassic Park*, intensifying as it echoed throughout the valley.

The kids looked at each other with bewilderment. Jimmy clutched the leg of his big sister.

"What was that?"

"I don't know." Patrick observed. "But it sounded angry."

He had the sensation of a field mouse caught out in the middle of a massive meadow, wandering where he shouldn't, underneath the unforgiving exposure of a full moon, it dawning on him he was vulnerable like an all you can eat Golden Coral buffet to any owl or hawk that was worth half it's feathers.

"I've never heard anything like that before." Rory remarked. "And I've been coming to this park my whole life."

The group passed around a set of worried looks.

"Let's get moving." Somebody said. "It's getting late."

It really wasn't. Or maybe it was but that wasn't why they said it.

The path brought them beyond the duck pond and emptied out into the guard rail of a dead end road.

"We're almost there." Spoke Patrick, the team's designated leader.

No one had briefed Rory or Jimmy about where they were headed but they had deduced that there was an actual destination to their travels and they were thankful for it now.

Alma Rodriguez's house was the third one on the left from the dead end. An immigrant herself, apparently her son had found some success in the Air Force and paid off her long time homestead in the working class side of Allenville. The abode rested on a somewhat steep hill at the top of a set of steps closer in resemblance to a ladder.

"OK, this is it." Whispered Patrick as he rested his hand on the aluminum gate to find it squeak open invitingly with little encouragement.

Maddy tilted her head back to take in the full scope of the dwelling. It looked about as hospitable as the *Amityville* manor.

"Whoa, man. I am not going up there and neither is Jimmy. There aren't even any lights on. I don't think anyone's home."

Patrick gestured with his eyes back towards the park where they had heard that spooky noise but it wasn't registering with Madison. She'd probably written it off as some random, nocturnal outcry. Amazing how one's mind contorts and acquiesces to convenience.

"I'll go." An easy opportunity for Rory to demonstrate his bravery.

"OK, come on. Are you sure you guys want to wait here? At least come inside the gate."

The boys made their way up the steps supported by a flimsy hand rail. Alma probably took full advantage of this. Plenty of natural pitfalls to keep nosey unwanteds and pesky solicitors away from her sanctuary. *I bet she doesn't even order a pizza,* Patrick thought. Old hermit ladies like her probably made their own from scratch. He wasn't old enough to know that that was usually a better alternative.

Once the duo reached the rickety porch of the one story flat, they could sense that something was wrong. No lights were on, not even the flicker of a TV screen. The door was wide open and the normally tidy screen was barely hanging off of it's hinges as though someone had forced their way through.

"Uh, hello? Ms. Alma? Mrs. Rodriguez?" Patrick knocked on the old wooden door panel.

That's when the foul stench became obnoxiously apparent. They curled their face in disgust and brought a hand to their noses. Rory brought his shirt over the bridge of his nose like a bandana and they started hacking.

"Ew, what is that?"

"I don't know. Her dog must've died under the porch or something and she hasn't smelled it from inside.

Ms. Alma! Are you OK?"

The longer they stayed, the more wrong the situation was becoming. Normally there would be a barrage of cats from all directions. Where were they?

Patrick went to knock on the door.....wide open.

"Ms. Alma!" He called out into the black. "We're coming in to check on you."

Rory's eyes bugged with disapproval.

"We are?"

"Rory, we've got to check on her. She's old."

Patrick contorted himself around the tenuously hanging screen door and slid his way inside with the finesse of a mongoose. He leaned forward on one set of toes, feeling on the wall for the light switch and nearly fell over from the weight of his friend colliding into his back.

"Sorry."

"Watch where you're going, you clumsy oaf. Hey, flick the lights on."

"I can't see anything."

"Give me your cigarette lighter."

"Here."

Patrick struggled with the poorly constructed device, striking it a good seven or eight times. Then it finally ignited and a thin halo where the boys stood flickered to life. The floor was coated with a green film, somewhat resembling Nickelodeon Gak. They grimaced at the sight.

"What is this stuff?" Rory petitioned.

"I don't know. Here, try the light switch."

Rory flicked it up and down several times. Nothing.

"Come on. Let's go."

"What about Ms. Alma?"

Patrick pivoted his head to answer his friend, replied with certainty, "She's dead."

Rory knew he was right. How wasn't important, he just wanted to be back in his messy room. So what if there were roaches and rats and moths and a peanut butter sandwich under his bed from three months ago? It was his home. It was his lair. And it was safe. No one would bother him there, not even his parents, though sometimes he might have wanted them to. Even if he had read all the comic books there, he'd gladly read them again. Anything to just get away from this infernal night.

CHAPTER 9

"But what about the children?" Challista pleaded from the passenger seat in that classic appeal to prudence.

Barry had been doing everything he could to keep from driving frantically. It's been said not to drive when one is emotional and now he could see why. In reality, he was driving around looking for answers because he wasn't totally sure which direction First Memorial Allenville Hospital was, even though he was more than familiar with the layout of the township.

"The gym is locked. They'll be fine. They can wait. Right now, I'm worried about your health."

"No! Barry! Please, don't take me. I'm much better. I was just on my period. That's why I was bleeding."

"I'm not stupid, Challista. I've been around the block. You can't just tell me something about women's issues and expect me to just accept it at face value. Something was going on with you back there. Who are you? That wasn't my wife!"

Challista erupted with devastation, burying her head in her lap. Barry, casting accusatory glances downward between distracted glimpses at the demands of stop lights and traffic signs.

"No! You don't understand. I couldn't control myself."

"You couldn't control yourself? Oh, ok. Well, maybe I should go over to the projects after I drop you off and score myself a little baggie of black tar heroin. You know, because I can't control myself."

"Barry, it wasn't me. It was Gary."

Coleman slammed the sedan to a screeching halt. Something had connected and a light bulb had clicked on above his cranium.

"So, Gary's back." He pondered.

Fellow motorists were angrily leaning on their horns and swerving around them, a mere side note to the saga unfolding inside the cabin.

Challista continued, "He was looking for some kind of book."

Barry stared blankly at a fixed point somewhere on the horizon, trying to connect the dots. Someone in a black Honda CRV blared their horn a couple of times, pulled past the driver side window to hurl some obscenities and Barry reluctantly returned to Earth.

"Barry, honey. Where are we going?"

"I'm taking you to your mother's." He answered with finality.

He was calm now. He knew what he had to do.

Detective Rosicky leaned backed in his office swivel chair with the Chinese takeout, manipulating the fried rice with his chopsticks. *You know*, he thought, *I'm not Sherlock Holmes but you don't have to be a world class sleuth to deduce that this isn't the most effective way to shovel food into one's mouth*. He still used them, though. Must be the novelty of it. But the Chinese don't have the novelty of it, do they?

BRRRNGGG

Rosicky jumped at the sputtering ring of the rotary office phone on his desk, an avalanche of fried rice cascading all over his clip on tie. Some casualties are unavoidable, especially in this line of work. He scrambled for the brown bag Ping had delivered and fumbled through the Styrofoam and paper, searching for the fortune cookie. A superstitious man by nature, he wanted to reveal his fortune during the ensuing phone call. Maybe it could do something to color his view of whatever information was to come from the other end of the line. Yes, Detective Martin Rosicky had an important job and it could be considered highly unprofessional to allow the phone to go unanswered for four consecutive rings while he fished for a delectable, sugary treat. But he was of the mind that one just can't put a price on mojo. That is to say, if there is something you do, some kind of pregame ritual, some kind of jinx, a saying that you recite in your head, a lucky pair of shoes or hat you might wear that just seemed to put you in the zone, never question it. Never stray from it. Just go with it. Some athletes drink pickle juice before each game. But God works in mysterious ways and by such margins are playoff games decided. Final exams passed. Cold cases cracked.

With the familiar plastic ruffling sound of his fingers finally encountered his prize, he deftly snatched up the desert cookie, simultaneously slamming his other hand down on the receiver of the office phone, now on it's fifth ring, catapulting it up to eye level where it was keenly grabbed out of thin air in a choreographed and well-rehearsed display he'd become somewhat of an office legend for. Not to discount his track record for solved cases.

"Rosicky?"

"Yeah, shoot."

"This is Willard. I'm here at A.S.H."

"Right. Go ahead."

He'd mastered the art of sounding impatient when he really wasn't. Pulled apart the seam of the plastic wrapper containing the fortune cookie like a bag of chips as he responded to Willard's introduction, marveling at it as he let it showcase between his thumb and middle finger like a precious stone.

"Nothing."

Rosicky waited patiently for some elaboration. None came.

"Excuse me?" He prompted. Perhaps there

was a short in the phone board circuitry.

"That's right, nothing. No evidence."

The fortune cookie snapped in half, in no small part due to the vitriol of the moment. Rosicky took his feet off of the desk and leaned forward in disbelief.

"Finger prints? Foot prints? I mean, I don't want to tell you how to do your job or anything- "

"No, you heard me correctly. I replayed the video from four different angles in the hallway and all of the outdoor cameras as well. None of them were tampered with. Simon can be seen escorted to his cell yesterday at approximately 1608 hours and he simply never leaves. Neither the door or window show any signs of adulteration and the computers have been analyzed for malfunctions and viruses. The ventilation grate inside the cell measures 12"x9" and shows no sign of manipulation. I don't know what to make of it."

As Willard spoke, Det. Martin Rosicky, with the office phone cradled on his shoulder, pulled the two halves of the fortune cookie apart and retrieved the small white slip of paper. Blank. Flipped to the other side. Blank again.

Well, that's fitting. Not even any lottery numbers? Must be a defect or lack thereof, to be more precise. That a good enough answer for you, Mr. Professor? A big, fat, steaming pile of nothing. He was forced to admit, ultimately, that the message was painfully clear. You get no clues, no direction and no fortune. Only the unremarkable comforts of a lightly sweetened wafer.

Or could there be more to the omen than simply an absence of one? Martin examined the implication carefully in his mind's eye. His methods were anything but by the book. As with any decision he faced in life, be it large or small, he often diverted his decision making to an external source. Where many remained loyal to the ever popular "gut", his intuition relied on the alignment of his thoughts with that which was simultaneously heard or seen. If a young person rang a bicycle bell at precisely the same moment as he was hovering his finger over a certain row of lottery tickets he was considering, he might take it as a catalyst in making such a selection. Sometimes he would be vindicated with a noteworthy prize. Sometimes not. Thusly, he remained loyal to this stratagem. On more than one occasion, while serving a warrant for a bond forfeiture or parole violation or even during a rugged foot pursuit, Detective Rosicky, having encountered frustration, bent down and plucked a pinch of grass blades and then letting them fall to the ground where he stood. Whatever direction the grass blades seemed partial to, he would follow.

This, of course, was never discussed. A good magician never divulges their tricks of the trade. But it was by this method of reasoning Martin Rosicky used to meticulously analyze the blank slip of paper he continued to adjust between his fingers. After all, the very absence of a fortune could be seen as a clue in and of itself. It was not a denial of information. It was a confirmation of all information. Could this be the case that was completely and totally open to interpretation in every conceivable way? He sure hoped not. This is no ordinary case. This could be a major problem. Not just for his professional career but quite possibly his sanity too, not that he hadn't considered it before but now that he was facing it in reality.......

"I almost forgot, there is one thing. A canister of Nickelodeon Gak was discovered underneath his bunk. Remember that stuff?"

"Are you serious?"

He was assuming he was, you just can't make this stuff up. Please let now be the time for Deputy Willard to make an awkward attempt at humor.

"Like a heart attack. No finger prints on that either."

"Well, did you take it out and play with it at least?"

Willard scoffed, "I don't even have time to play with my own dick."

CHAPTER 10

When the boys reached the bottom of the steps, Rory began fidgeting through his pockets for his half smoked cigarette.

"Never too late to quit, you know?" Maddy quipped. "Not home, huh?"

The short fell out of his mouth as he attempted to respond. Patrick cut him off.

"Yeah, must be out running some errands. Looking for this?" He tossed Rory the cheap yellow lighter. It hit him square in the chest and bounced to the ground, altering his puzzlement.

"I wanna go home." Was the whimper from Jimmy.

"Yeah, me too. Sorry I wasted everyone's time. Jimmy, give me a candy for the road."

"Hold on, guys. I'm coming." The group had already gained some ground as he fiddled with the tobacco, eventually gave up as the distance increased.

The dark purple shade of sky shown clear, piercing through the night air as they neared the pond. A slight breeze was no match for an unusually amorous bull frog. Beneath croons, they could feel the crunch of the autumn leaves and dried foliage beneath their boots. Rory continued to fiddle with the lighter as he walked, the obstinacy of the device winding his course.

"Come on, Rory. I'm cold." Maddy called out from ahead.

Could she be trying to tell me something? His eyes widened as he cupped the short around the reluctant flint spark. *If I could just get this thing lit, I can complete my 'super cool' image.* He halted for a moment to focus his concentration, dipped out of the wind.

WHOOK

Fire.

Rory struggled through a breath of sophistication.

"Put that thing down. Aren't you going to keep me company?"

Maddy turned to check on the slowpoke and felt her jaw drop with befuddlement at the spectacle her mind struggled to comprehend. There. In the night sky. There could be no mistake of it. With the light from the innumerable stars, nebulas and galaxies, the heavens had been revealed with indubitable clarity. Something was......coming. Fast. From high up. The moon served as a majestic backdrop for the figure taking shape beyond her friend. It just wasn't a bird. *Oh, how I wish it was a bird.* Far too large, though. And maneuverable. Too early for Santa, so no chance for that. No. Somewhere in her young and innocent mind, she knew. It's amazing how kids or certain people know some things. They don't have the training or certifications. No experience or memories to guide them. No voice in their head or ancient ancestor whispering hints in their ears. Not necessarily. They just know. And their conviction is unwavering. And they are usually right.

By this means did Madison Henley make some sort of connection with in her being. This is why she wanted to scream. Even though she couldn't. No matter how hard she tried. Because she was petrified with fear. No one had ever warned her beforehand to keep her eyes open or maintain awareness for what she was witnessing. It was as if a primeval instinct buried deep within her genealogy, ingrained like grooves in a record through intense pressure and duress, never to be erased, always to be preserved and concealed until it's eventual use, no matter how improbable.

The winged visage fluttered, dipped and swooped in stuttered waves from the position of the moon in the foreground. The waves increased in size as it drew closer. It must have been powerful too, in order to support all of that weight and still remain airborne.

Maddy could hear herself screaming from inside her body for some time now. She wanted so desperately to do something for her friend. To warn him. To at least give him a chance. Only timid whimpers were squeaking out. Jimmy noticed her cessation and had returned to her side in the familiar, protective umbrella of her shadow where he continued perusing through his collection, oblivious. More sounds were emerging from her throat now. Her vocal chords were beginning to grab the syllables more effectively.

"uh.........uh........oh........OOOHHH! OOO-OOOOHHHHH! OOOOOOOOHHHHH!"

She finally managed to exclaim, her finger hanging in the air, indicating the direction of her angst. Her mind was too shocked to fully vocalize words yet but it was enough to alert Patrick to her plight. He'd approached her side with a quizzical expression, his eyes searching for the slice of sky she was trying to alert to.

Rory was concerned now. But there was just no way for him to have pieced together what was happening. He was trotting over to Maddy. Originally, it seemed like a prank or something. He was enjoying the attention. It had appeared she was pointing at him at first. But now that he was much closer, he could sense the seriousness of the situation. His smile was gone now as he gathered the courage to turn around and find the source of his friends awe. He could tell by the horror on her face that he was not going to like what was awaiting him. Yet, he knew there was no avoiding it. He closed his eyes and prayed to wake up from a bad dream. Once you know you're dreaming, you can wake up if your will power is strong enough. Everyone knows that.

"RUN!!! RUN!!!"

The urgent exhortations ruined his private requests for a reality check. He couldn't simply just comply with the commands, even though he knew that he should. Curiosity was getting the better of him now, he willed his eyes open and instantly regretted doing so.

The creature's massive wings sliced through the air as they beat out impressive strokes.

WHOOPF

WHOOPF

WHOOPF

WHOOPF

There was no time to process things. A Shamu sized dose of adrenaline surged though his veins, giving way to a Fred Flintstone like spin out of tennis shoes from beneath him. Once the grooves on the bottom of his sneakers took hold of the earth, he was too frightened to realize just how fast he was sprinting, if his feet were even touching the ground at all as if propelled by pure panic.

Rory had closed the gap between himself and his friends with astonishing quickness. You never know how fast you truly are until your life is in danger. No one had ever considered him suitable for athletic activities before but if there were any talent scouts watching from some concealed perspective, they would surely have been clamoring for an interview. His eyes wide like dinner plates, threatening to break from their respective cheek bones with alarm, he tore through the wilderness, unwittingly clawing past his comrades, gaining further momentum by heaving himself past their seemingly motionless bodies.

Maddy was especially gifted for her age. With the hormonal head start of adolescence most young women receive, her advantage apparent as she strode effortlessly past Patrick, no slouch in the wind sprint department himself, perhaps still reacting more from the testimony of his buddies than what he'd witnessed firsthand. He was well aware of the magnetic frequency of terror transmitted from his cohorts.

After the initial burst of adrenaline however, Maddy was coming to an awful realization, stopping her in her tracks.

"Oh, no. Jimmy!"

The unfortunate epiphany hit Madison like a ton of bricks. She turned quickly at this, her eyes scanning for the little red Power Ranger costume which housed the boy. Patrick had instinctively halted at her alarm. A part of him had to have known there was no way the little tyke could possibly keep up with the older kids in an all-out sprint.

There he is! In the murky environment of the meadow they found themselves in, Jimmy's tiny frame could be made out, booking toward them as fast as his little legs could carry him yet still a substantial distance back from the group. Maddy was frozen with indecision. She observed her body stunned with incapability from a third person point of view as shock began to take hold of her mind's ability to function under the unusual circumstances. The beast was swooping down, it's wings pinned back for increased velocity like a Peregrine falcon in dive bomber mode, preparing to snatch Jimmy up like a drive through order doggy bag, payment a distant afterthought.

SCREEEEEEEE

The creature emitted a ferocious, high pitched squeal as it bore down on young Jimmy, extending it's well-muscled arms to reveal powerful claws, the moon light glinting off of their tips. It is in moments like these where serendipity lies. Although the defenseless Jimmy had seemingly no chance to evade the winged predator, opportunity came to the rescue in the nick of time. Whether the darkness, the chaos of the moment or Jimmy's awkward gait, made lopsided by his insistence on running with his teddy bear and plastic pail, flailing and sending candy flying in all directions, a root or crevice had sprung before him just enough to suck his body into the Earth in one fluid motion.

The timing couldn't have been more favorable. The monster hissed with disappointment as it clutched at vacant space. It was moving far too rapidly in its descent to have landed or do anything else but swoop high back into the atmosphere to recover it's bearings without the 2nd grader cargo it had calculated to have had in it's grasps.

SCREEEEEE

SCREEEEEE

It veered out and to the left in a football field sized loop, its wingspan stretched wide in the 'gliding' position as it coasted with sheer inertia. Jimmy bleated desperately at the hysteria of the moment. A part of him must have been aware of how close he'd actually come to death. Big sister's maternal instincts had finally kicked in and she made a motion towards the youngster, pushing off the gravel, vegetation crunching beneath her treads.

"Jimmy!" She screamed.

He'd picked himself up, gathered his bear and began stumbling towards the location of the still stunned group, the candy less of a priority now. Maddy moved to close the gap between them, no more than twenty yards at this point.

With resounding quickness, their winged tormentor appeared from the peripheral and forcefully planted it's massive feet into the supple earth with a mighty impact, interjecting itself between them menacingly. It snorted in satisfaction with its landing. Maddy's feet betrayed her as she fell backwards, propping herself up on her palms in respect to the sinister barrier having suddenly been erected before her. The beast stood before her with it's wings open and it's hands on it's hips, a devilish smirk spread across it's face as it relished the dissolution of it's victim's reunion, it's long, forked tongue wagging with excitement.

What *was* it?

WHAT THE HELL IS IT???

When she'd first caught sight of it, the only thing her mind she could come up with was it must be some kind of outrageously large bat. She didn't have time to even attempt to conjecture about where it came from or, for that matter, how it had come into existence. Perhaps some kind of freakish, Godzilla style, failed nuclear reactor energy experiment gone wrong. That's easy. The bat had settled down next to a hemorrhaging uranium refinery. Or, who knows? She was young. Who's to say there wasn't some exotic locality where abnormally large, man size bats were the norm. But now that it was standing directly in front of her, there was no mistaking it for a bat. What could she compare it to? Nothing. A demon maybe or the personification of what one might imagine from the third dimension. If anything, some kind of gargoyle at least. Whatever it was, it was big. It's human form might remind someone of an extraordinarily robust linebacker. The animal must've been at least 450lbs. It seemed to be content to simply act as an impasse, allowing the young woman to soak in the horror.

But it had grown tired of the 'show and tell' game. It began to step closer to her. She was helpless in the situation, caught between two minds. If she ran, she'd abandon her brother to its whims. If she stayed, there was little resistance she could afford, she'd be diced to mincemeat with ease. The gargoyle towered over her, savoring every moment of her paralysis. A grin of amusement spread across it's face, revealing rows of dagger like teeth, as it inched closer to it's prey. The beast unexpectedly winced with annoyance as a fist sized rock thudded into its head.

"Take that you fucking freak!" Rory yelled as he emerged between it and his love interest.

He produced another stone with soft ball like dimensions and hurled it at the monster's maw from point blank range.

SCREEEEEEE

The beast shrieked with pain as the projectile made contact with it's upper lip. It proceeded to rear back its sizable paw and brought it down across poor Rory's head like a tiger's maul. Rory was thrust to the ground ungracefully, his face obscured with red. He didn't even get a chance to scream.

Jimmy and Madison had wisely used the intervention to capitalize on the distraction created by their friend and were now reaching the end of the park, shepherded by Patrick. They'd reached the home neighborhood before they realized the predator wasn't following them like they thought it might be. Surely, they were thinking about Rory. But they all seemed to know there was no point in wondering if he was ok. He was gone now. The significance of his sacrifice was not lost on them. He'd given his short life to save theirs. At least he'd died quickly. They hoped.

CHAPTER 11

Pastor Coleman rolled up the window to focus more intently on his inner dialogue. A hideous squeal had pierced through the night as he cruised through Challista's mother's neighborhood, disrupting his train of thought. *Is the whole world going mad? Bunch of hooligans, even if it is Halloween. Goddamn stupid pagan holiday anyway. No wonder God has been seeing to the destruction of this country. Must be furious, observing from his celestial abode.*

Now that Challista was safe at her mother's, he could turn his attention to the new and unsettling information. Gary Simon was back and he wanted The Book. Barry was trying to revisit his memories, hoping to understand how it had come into his possession. Although he had pushed his actions concerning The Book to the back burner at the time, maybe it would give him perspective on what to do next.

He'd wandered from the administrative area of the church ground on a particularly uneventful Wednesday during his office hours to the sanctuary in order to clear his mind and perhaps offer a prayer in front of the altar, only to discover an old man sitting alone in the middle of the pews. He'd taken the time to light a number of candles which at first Coleman had found a bit pretentious but upon closer examination of the old man, excusable given the harmless and overall agreeable countenance he seemed to exude. Coleman had crept up from the entrance and when he noticed the man was not in prayer but simply sitting patiently, he placed a hand on one of the book stops next to the aisle and introduced himself. The old man calmly stood up, walked over to the aisle and addressed the church leader.

"My name is Giovanni Bernard."

He was dressed in a brown vintage suit with an unassuming, soft toned yellow and gold dress shirt and tie beneath. Well-tailored, with both hands he held a bowler hat close to his body. When his gray eyes met Barry's, he fell into a trance state.

Apparently, he'd come quite a distance and traveled at great length to see Barry. His gentle cadence and compassionate gaze relaxed Barry and he felt assured and safe in the elder man's presence. Strangely, he appeared to already know Pastor Coleman's name.

"You are a good man, Pastor Coleman. You are responsible and you care about your flock."

He mentioned this with a hint of satisfaction, an implied smile forming at the corner of his mouth. Barry felt it a peculiar observation for a stranger to make but couldn't come up with a counterpoint. He knew he'd done his very best. He'd made a comfortable living for himself and his family but he wasn't like some of these mega church leaders, vacationing in their yachts, giving sermons to stadium seating audiences.

"I have something for you."

You do? What could it be? For me? No one ever thinks to bring me a gift during office hours.

"Over by the pulpit. Go, look." He gestured with his hypnotizing, grey eyes.

Barry serenely stepped over to the familiar pulpit where he had delivered so many sermons over the years and peered into the cavern of the podium. He bent down and recovered a small, wooden chest. Displayed it on the podium and took a step back to appreciate it.

"Thank you, Giovanni."

Giovanni opened his arms and spread wide his hands in a revelatory motion.

"Open it. Look inside."

Barry could see a powerful white light shining from inside the chest, escaping through some of the cracks in the woodwork. He carefully lifted open the top and pushed it back on its hinges. The light was blinding. It was so pure it could be said to have been the very absence of color. It radiated from within the chest, casting rays throughout the sanctuary chamber, igniting the stained glass cherubs, giving life to the vibrant colors. Barry winced, inundated by the glare.

"Don't be afraid. Go ahead. Reach inside."

He mustered courage from within and guided his eyes into the bright. When they returned, in them rested a beautiful, leather bound book. The source of the majestic radiance could be seen to originate from the skillfully embroidered oak tree symbol on its face. It was breathtaking. An antiquity of exceptional quality. Coleman returned to the gaze of the strange man, seeking approval. Giovanni had taken up a position adjacent to him in the worship area.

"Pastor Coleman, I have chosen you to accept this sacred Book of the Ages. I have protected it for many years. Now I have grown old and it is time for me to go home now. Barry, I want you to take good care of this parchment. I want you to hide it. Put it somewhere only you know. Somewhere it will be safe. This is a very important book for this village and this realm. Will you do this task for me?"

Coleman weighed his options and considered the mysterious man's proposition. It seemed like quite a large favor to ask of someone, especially someone you'd just met five minutes ago. However, Barry felt strangely comforted by the proposal. He didn't feel pressured, although one could easily point out that he'd been put on the spot. He didn't feel burdened with the magnanimity of the request. Even now, the large print book, easily 1,200 pages, felt light as a feather in his grasp.

"Yes."

The affirmation was met with a broad smile by the old man. Barry returned his attention to the compendium, marveling at its purity.

"Just what is the nature of this record?" He asked.

He looked up, searching for the familiarity of those smoky, grey eyes but they were gone.

"Giovanni?"

He twirled around, checked his blind spots.

Was I dreaming? Did I just have a midday hallucination? I was just rubbing my eyes in my office a minute ago.

But he was still holding The Book. The chest was still there.

O.K., what's the catch? Where's the gimmick? He strode from corner to corner, checking under each pew. He checked the bathrooms, the offices, the gymnasium and eventually the parking lot. Ok, no cars. This guy had seriously booked. He didn't exactly carry the portrayal of athleticism with that full, blonde and gray beard. Mostly gray. But you know, some of those older guys run marathons in their spare time. He was definitely in a hurry to get the heck out of dodge, wasn't he? *Wonder if he stole something. Oldest trick in the book, right? 'Here, sir. Take this magic book while I hit the safe.' Ooh! What a hustle!*

Coleman was forced to confront himself when he returned to the altar where the chest lay open, the book next to it. *Must be some crazy man. A homeless person or something. Probably an entire lifetime of rants and raves and endless stories with no plot, no resolution. Here, father. Take my life's works. It's my memoirs. Don't ask me who I am. Gotta be going now! O.K., job well done. Time to hit the liquor store! Just what is this Godforsaken book?*

He unlatched the leather bind, folded over the cover.

Manifest

Official
Records of Heaven

the names of these contained
herein
are to be admitted through
the Pearly Gates
on the Day of Reckoning
on a date in time to be
determined by God

St. Peter,
Apostle of Jesus Christ

The letters glittered and gleamed with golden calligraphy.

Whatever. Ok. Let me just thumb through the leaflets and....the names, were actual people in Allenville. He and Challista were listed. Their children. Their children's children. A number of friends and family members, acquaintances. *Now that's dedication and attention to detail! What'd he do; copy a bunch of names out of the telephone book?*

Something inside him told him to knock it off with the sarcasm. He couldn't deny it, the clues added up. God works in mysterious ways. You can't live by that phrase and then question it when things are mysterious. Sure. But he wasn't in a hurry to get hoodwinked either.

Barry returned the book to it's resting place in the chest and carried it back to his office. Once there, he placed the chest underneath his desk, removed the book and set it on the desk in front of him. He steepled his fingers, brought them to his chin as he combed through his mind trying to decide where to hide the book.

CHAPTER 12

Maddy finally began to accept that she was going to survive when she caught sight of the familiar red door which trademarked the Henley family compound. With Patrick next to her, she charged over the lawn with Jimmy in tow, his other hand still hanging on determinately to the bear. She could feel the emotion swelling through her as she made the final steps and finally burst through the portal, exploding into a cacophony of hysterics.

Patrick comforted her while Jimmy curled up in a ball next to his sister, emotionally and mentally drained. She wept uncontrollably, struggling to process the new reality she had unwittingly stepped into. Everything had happened so fast. One minute, Rory was here. With them. Gathering candy like every other normal school child. The next, gone. Clubbed by a brute in front of his friends. There was no reason to think he could've survived. Even if he had, who's to know what had transpired there between them after they'd fled. The creature's claws had perforated Rory's supple shell with such ferocity.....oh! The very thought was gut wrenching.

The events of the night had unfolded with such velocity, they now found themselves passively existing in the Henley's veranda. They hadn't even had a chance to process their experience between themselves, let alone get their stories straight. Which was important now because rumbling's, shifts of weight and sounds of furniture rattling, lights flickering on indicated the Henley's had been rousted from their respective dream lands.

This is a problem. And it was beginning to dawn on Patrick as to why: HOW IN THE WORLD WERE THEY GOING TO EXPLAIN THIS? If they told the truth; the consequences could be exceptionally unbeneficial. What if no one believed them? What if someone painted them out to be crazy? What if they accused them of foul play? Indeed, what self-respecting law enforcement agency is going to issue an A.P.B. on a 400lb gargoyle?

Any chance they had of conferencing was over now though, as Bob came thundering down the stairs.

"Madison! What is it? What's going on?" He demanded as he vaulted down the last steps and knelt next to her with a hand on her back, coaxing her.

"Oh, daddy. (sniff) He's dead, daddy! He's de-ead!"

"Who. Who's dead?"

"Rory. He's gone!"

Patrick watched with wide eyes as Maddy proceeded to spill the beans. Cut her a break, he thought, considering what they'd been through. Whatever. He couldn't expect them to lie about it forever. Only thing to do now: bite the bullet. Who knows? The way things had been going, at this rate someone might actually be inclined to believe them.

"What happened?" Robert's expression changed to anger.

Was this another prank? Because it isn't funny. Besides, he was just here. In my care. If that little fuck up did go and overdose, they better not come trying to blame me!

"Daddy. Oh, daddy." She just kept shaking her head in denial.

The seasoned father of fourteen years softened his tone. "Maddy, baby. It's ok. I'm your father. You can tell me anything. Go on." His eyes filled with concern.

Maddy sniffed, wiped her nose on her sleeve and met her father's gaze.

"Dad. Please, believe me. It was this monster. Like a giant bat." She whimpered, her bottom lip quivering.

At this, Mr. Henley snapped like a twig. "God damn it, this is not funny anymore! Who is behind this?" He turned his attention to Patrick. "Was it you?"

Patrick shrunk back from the accusing finger Madison's dad had thrust his direction.

"No sir, Mr. Henley." He managed to eke out.

"I don't like what you're doing to my daughter, you and your doped up friend! You get the hell out of my house and you leave her alone, you understand?"

Patrick looked over to Maddy for help.

"No, daddy! He didn't do anything. I'm telling you the truth. Why don't you believe me?"

"Madison, are you using drugs? Is there something you want to tell me? I'm not stupid, you know. I've been fourteen before too."

"What's going on? Honey?" Linda descended down the stairs, clutching her nightgown.

Bob sighed at this. Well, no chance at sweeping this under the rug and moving on with life. This was a thing now. Mrs. Henley engulfed her daughter in an embrace, placing her hands on her cheeks and forehead. Did she have a fever?

"James, go upstairs. What's happening?"

"Maddy's idiot friends are taking things too far. Earlier they were over here, fainting from whatever drugs they're on, talking about devils and what not. Now, they've got her playing some kind of prank and I don't fucking like it! Crying wolf about a monster eating the other dumb ass and I think they may have given her something too." Bob summarized with his hands on his hips.

"Oh, for Pete's sake." She was brushing her only daughter's hair. "You know, if I were to pull this crap when I was your age, my parents would've sent me to a boarding school."

"No!" Young Madison erupted at her mother's dismissal, burying her head into clasped handed.

The two parental units looked at each other with confusion. Why was she being so dramatic? Probably teenage hormone overload. She shifted her attention to her younger son, kissed him on the forehead, pointing upstairs. "Come on, Jimmy. Let's get ready for bed."

Patrick had already begun inching towards the door.

That's right. Keep it moving, buddy. Man, I cannot wait to get these little punks out of my house and out of my life.

Thrust into the cold evening wind minus one friend, his credibility under scrutiny and the threat of an unknown terror still lurking, Patrick's head spun with an overwhelming sensation. He'd seen what had happened. They all had. It looked like adults weren't going to be a help with this problem. He'd paid attention in school but where was the text book on gargoyle evasion tactics? Going to the police struck him as an egregiously reckless move. *Where is your friend? You don't say? How did that happen? Oh, really? Or is it more likely you and your little friends did away with him? Was it jealousy? About the girl?* Patrick was a safe bet for the juvenile corrections facility, if they didn't try him as an adult at that or commitment to the asylum at the very least.

Patrick coaxed himself off the porch and debated whether to take cover in some nearby hedges. He wished to go back to the park. He wanted desperately to avenge Rory. He wanted to hunt the creature down and kill it viciously, the same way it did to his friend. But he knew he couldn't. There was nothing to be done. He didn't like the feeling of helplessness. It reminded him of his days getting picked on by the older kids. He reached in his pocket and grabbed the cell phone his parents had given him for emergencies.

CHAPTER 13

Flashing red, white and blue lights intercepted Pastor Coleman's attention and jerked him out of his flashback as he slid the luxury sedan smoothly around the corner of a four way stop, the tires crackling in tandem with the moist gravel from the light drizzle.

Oh, my God. Am I getting pulled over?

The sensation makes everyone's cheeks clench regardless of criminal sophistication. On a subconscious level, everyone knows it's over when they see those lights illuminating the cabin panels and twinkling in their rearview. Some who've run have made it. Most haven't. It's a headache to consider either way. And people know, whether they want to admit it or not, they have you. If they want to take full advantage of you, they can. At the very least, there will be punitive damages.

But the lights weren't coming from behind him, thank Heavens. The parking lot on the corner. It was the church parking lot. His church. *Was I that lost in my thoughts?*

Lord!

No. Could something have happened to one of the children while I was gone?

Coleman pulled the vehicle into the parking lot and landed next to the handful of cars huddled together near the middle. A man and woman stood with their arms folded, chatting with a police officer. As he jumped out of the Buick and approached the conference, Larry Perkins alerted them to his presence.

"Look, there he is now."

"What's going on?"

Coleman searched their eyes for answers. The cop was first to reply.

"Just a welfare check, Pastor Coleman. Half an hour ago, this parking was full of parents and children."

"Oh, yes. My wife fell ill. I took her home." He explained it away, though his expression betrayed the severity of the moment.

"Praise be to God." Chimed Bethany Simpson. "We feared the worst when you didn't answer your phone."

Oh, yeah. I have a cell phone. The concept had escaped him during the preceding chaos of the events still unfolding.

"Thank you, Bethany. Everything's quite fine. I'm sorry to inconvenience everyone. I just wanted to get Challista somewhere safe."

Larry stepped in as one of his twins latched on to his leg. "Sorry to give you a start, Barry. It was just so strange to come back after we talked and find you gone and the doors unlocked and wide open.”

“They were? Oh, no. I always carefully lock the doors before I shut down. I remember doing it, even as Challista went to the car.”

“Actually, all the doors were open. The gym, the activity hall, office area, kitchen and even the sanctuary. The class rooms were open too.”

Barry grimaced. *What next?*

“Should we take a look around?” Offered the law man. His name plate read Smith 1845.

“Um, yeah.” Coleman nodded in agreement. “We’d better make sure no one’s taken the offertory or anything else.”

“Gosh, Barry. I hope everything’s ok. I’d help you lock the place back up but I need to get these kiddos home.” Larry compensated. “Looks like you’re in the capable hands of Allenville’s finest, anyway.” He walked over and gave Barry a warm hug. “ I’m glad you’re ok, brother. I’ll call you tomorrow.”

“Absolutely, Larry. Thanks. That goes for you too, Beth. You can go ahead and go home. Get out of this weather before you catch a cold.”

“Oh, no. Really, it’s alright. Let me help you. I’m not doing anything right now. Is Challista ok?”

“Uh, yes. I think she’ll be fine.”

Coleman was already walking briskly toward the side door to the office area. All the perimeter doors would need to be checked and locked again.

If someone had raided the safe, the money was insured but there would be paperwork. He sighed with the realization of the tedium his near future had in store for him. Wait. Why was he going about it like this? *Oh, yeah. My wife was raped. Well, here's your chance to make a report to the police. Of course, I didn't actually see Gary. But my wife wouldn't lie to me. Would she?* Besides, The Book was the important thing right now.

"No really, Mrs. Simpson. That won't be necessary. I'm just going to finish up with Officer Smith here and get back to my wife." He stammered as they entered the building.

She just wouldn't take no for an answer. "It's ok. Let me help you. I'll lock the classroom doors and the activity rooms." She insisted.

Pastor Coleman continued with Smith to the office area undeterred. Hopefully the church proceeds were still intact, the safe contained a substantial amount of cash. A big trip to Central America had been in the works. They arrived at the office to discover the door open and an ugly mess waiting inside. Papers were strewn. Drawers had been ransacked. Barry rushed to the safe, twisted in the combination and flung the door open. As expected, empty.

"I suppose you'll want to make a report." Officer Smith broke in.

"You got that right."

Coleman was shaking his head at the failure of human decency. *Really? Robbing the church? Any-*

time now, Lord. The end must be near. If I were God, he mused, *I'd have pulled the plug a long time ago. Thank God, I'm not! Thank God for his awesome mercy.*

He crouched under the desk and checked the small wooden chest with the white tree symbol emblazoned. Wide open. Surprise, surprise. At least no one had The Book. That much he knew. He'd ingeniously stowed it away months ago where no one would ever think to search for it.

Pastor Coleman suddenly felt uncomfortable. Somebody's eyes were on him. It was Officer Smith.

"Uh, did you want to go ahead and get the paperwork started, Officer Smith?"

Smith had been standing with his hands in his pockets, monitoring Coleman. It's rude to stare.

"Oh, yes. The paperwork. Right."

Coleman paused and settled himself into question answering mode. Only they weren't coming for some reason. Actually, no attempt was being made on Officer Smith's part to produce a notepad or anything of that nature. There were several blank legal pads clearly visible on the desk. No one was making a motion to pick them up. Creepy.

A sound emanated from the hallway. Wheels. A cart or something. Drawing closer, making the awkward silence between Smith and Coleman all the more unsettling.

Bethany appeared outside the door in the

hallway with a bright yellow, plastic mop bucket in tow, guiding it by an orange handled dollar store mop. Petite, standing at 5'2", the French braided, pale skinned Bethany Simpson cinched her cashmere sweater closed and smiled approvingly at the duo. She seemed to be content with the discomfort in the air.

Barry Coleman returned his gaze back to Officer Smith. With the anticlimax of the night's events, perhaps he hadn't noticed them before, Smith's piercing, bright amethyst eyes. He smiled at Coleman's realization, revealing a set of fangs.

The jig was up. Coleman felt the adrenaline rush as he dashed for the doorway. He had no idea the conspiracy ran this deep!

Mrs. Simpson met him there with the end of the mop stick, driving it into his gut. Surprisingly strong for her frame, the blow promptly removed the wind from Barry's diaphragm as he crouched over the stick, eyes bulging, bringing his hands to his stomach. He stumbled backward into his office, trying to regain his breath, still hunching over from the pain, half expecting the psycho cop to catch him. Instead, Coleman brought his vision up to find Officer Smith coolly removing his baton from his utility belt. His perception turned to black at that time as Smith brought the baton down on the back of Barry's hapless noggin.

When her parents finally left her room, Madison buried her head deep into her pillow.

Well, maybe if she pressed the issue and stuck to her story or perhaps altered it slightly to make it more presentable, she could convince her folks to look further into the incident in the morning. She had to do something for her friend. She had to do something for Rory.

Bob and Linda were concerned for their daughter but Jimmy's corroboration of her account had softened their stance considerably. It was all too sudden for them to accept these impressionable young people's story but they had resolved to 'sleep on it'. Why do they always want to sleep on it? When kids have a nightmare or a strange dream, it is quickly explained away as just a dream, not real. So why, when any decision of import comes into play, is it necessary to consult the dream realm for clarity? Surely, the same variables would still apply when they arise next morning.

Regardless, even if they were still unwilling to help, she was smart enough to know, if you don't deal with your problems, you can't expect them to go away on their own. And a 400lb gargoyle is one hell of a problem. And it was still out there. And so was Patrick. Sleep was a forgone conclusion.

Maddy's mind spun consistently like the Energizer Bunny in a hamster wheel. She must have been working herself into a fit for at least 45 minutes before she noticed the incandescent glow coming from beneath her bed.

Dear Lord, please let this be a dream and I could just wake up from this and go back to bed. She willed her eyes open, pulled the covers from where she'd been holding them on her sandy blonde head of hair and was disappointed to find the eerie light still reflecting off of the ceiling. The glow was accompanied by a chime which modulated with intensity as the light rose and fell.

The apparition wasn't going anywhere. There was something she was supposed to see.

I can do this. I'm in my bed. In my house. If I don't face this, there will be nowhere I can go for safety, especially with that thing out there.

Young Madison Henley bravely forced herself to peer over the edge of the mattress and let her head hang so she could locate the source of the brightness. Most people equate light with love, positivity, purity. The line of thinking lead Maddy to hope there was serendipity awaiting her. But this light wasn't exactly white. It was dirty. A yellowish, green color with all the mood of a fast food restaurant tile floor. What met her eyes was equally disturbing. It was her friend. Or more accurately, what was left of him. Rory's disfigured remains lay in a gory heap underneath the wooden frame of her sleeping area. Very little skin was still visible. A mélange of ripped flesh, bone, torn muscle fibers and vital organs, bloodied to a pulp composed the amalgam of what was once Rory Sieverson. His hollowed out eye sockets held a pair of sparks bearing the same type of light which illuminated his body. This was seemingly the source of the light.

Madison shrunk back under the covers and shuddered at the abysmal imagery. She gripped the covers tightly over her eyes, trying to come up with a prayer or creed she could repeat over and over until it went away but she was too scared to come up with anything. Not even the Lord's prayer. She was too frightened to scream even. *If I scream*, she reasoned, *who knows what would happen next?* It might do nothing more than galvanize whatever visage that was accosting her in her own dwelling. How was she to know that she might not drag her parents into some kind of serious, supernatural threat anyway? An impressively mature rumination, given the circumstances. If whatever it was was already in her bedroom and she may or may not become a casualty, why add her dear mum and dad to the talley?

Unfortunately, an unsettling sound broke up her thoughts. The mass of guts and tissue began gurgling and bubbling. *Oh, my God! Could he still be alive?* Maddy's face fell full of contempt. She summoned the courage to look back underneath the bed. Rory's eyes fixed on her as if he were waiting for her to return.

"Maa-maaaaddy." It murmured. "Maa-aa-aaadddy." He stretched a putrid hand toward her, searching for relief.

Somehow, she felt, she knew, she wasn't in danger presently.

"No, Rory. You're dead now. It's ok. You can rest now."

"Maaa-aa-aaady. Help me. Helllp me."

Maddy jolted awake in her bed at the sound of something scratching at her window. No weird glow. No glob-o-guts. It was a dream. She was panting and sweating.

TAP

TAP

TAP

Patrick's face hovered in the corner of the window.

Maddy hopped out of bed and hurried over to the window, unlatched it, raised it up a couple of feet. It was heavy but she was aware of it's dimensions. Patrick slid inside head first and rolled forward deftly on to the carpet without making so much as a noise.

"Hey, are you ok?" She whispered.

Patrick regained his breath, "Yeah."

He picked himself up and they shared a heart-felt embrace.

"I was worried about you."

"I was too." He confessed. "I was going to call my mom but I didn't want to go home. I don't want my mom to be driving around out here with that thing on the loose."

"Yeah, I understand. I'm glad you stuck around. I was kind of hoping you had some good news or something, like it was all a bad dream."

Patrick looked at the ground at this. It was

not a bad dream. It was real.

"I want to do something about it. I don't like sitting around and waiting for that thing to find us. I want to do something about Rory. What if he's ok? We have to do something because no one else is going to."

Maddy looked into his eyes and knew he was right.

"Ok........but what are we supposed to do? What can we do?"

The question was met with silence.

"I don't know. I think it can bleed, just like you and me. You saw when Rory hit it in the face with that rock, didn't you?"

She nodded.

"It didn't like that."

Maddy reflected for a moment.

"Hmm. Ok, I have an idea. Wait here."

Patrick waited in the dark for about fifteen minutes. When Madison returned, she had a brown and black Adidas shoe box. She placed it on the ground between them and popped the box top off. What lay inside was too good to be true. To Patrick, it looked about as good as a tall stack of pancakes and large glass of ice water after traveling through the Gobi for three days on foot with no supplies. Patrick reached into the box of rags, removed a big, black Ruger .380 snub nose revolver. Patrick lightly ran his fingers across it as though it was the most delicate, dainty woman to walk the Earth.

"You gotta be kidding me."

"He's been drinking tonight. I knew I could sneak around in the dark and grab it. He doesn't even know I know he has it. Here, take these."

She dumped a handful of shells into his palm. Hollow tip: when you care enough to send the very best. Big Bob didn't exactly consider himself a firearms enthusiast, we find ourselves in a blue state. But he felt that if he was confronted with the possibility of someone intruding into his homestead with his family asleep, he wanted to be sure they would go down if he hit. The next guy might think twice about it.

"Do you know how to use that?"

Patrick eyed the device. He'd always wanted to play cops and robbers. A childhood spent simulating cowboys and Indians show-downs with finger pistols or even running some Nerf gun war games with his friends had given him to imagine a day where he might play out the scenarios in real life as though he was garnering some actual training hours during those scrimmages. But this was a little more serious than he had envisioned. His best friend wasn't supposed to be dead. Especially at the hands of a supernatural, mythological beast no one else seemed to believe even existed, giving it the ultimate element of surprise. The shadow of doubt even causing him to toy with the notion, briefly, was he in a dark, twisted mausoleum of the mind which merely seemed real to him and him alone? Who's to say.

When that crazy man is shouting about space aliens on the street corner, they certainly seem real to *him*.

Hmm, I guess it's supposed to have a safety. He turned it over from side to side. No safety. It's a revolver. He mistook for the latch, unlocking the cylinder. Feeling it adjust, he slid the button to the side and unfolded the cylinder. Five slots, five bullets. He carefully clicked each slug into it's respective chamber and rolled the cylinder back into place, the gratifying click signifying it was locked in.

"Um, yes." He replied unconvincingly. "Let's go back to the field. I'm going to kill that thing."

CHAPTER 14

Barry Coleman slowly regained consciousness, awakening to a blurry, hazy world, mired with a hangover like fuzziness. He blinked in disbelief, swallowed in an attempt to gain saliva. He was parched. He found himself spread eagled, bound to the table in the middle of the altar area where he had prepared so many communion rituals over the years. The sanctuary was colored with a demonic shade of red as the lights from numerous candles danced from all directions.

Coleman adjusted his senses to process the sights and sounds occurring in and around him.

"Unh. Unhhh. What's happening? What are you doing to me?" He moaned.

Officer Smith, no longer in full uniform, wearing a white crew cut t-shirt, was hunched over, limping around excitedly, working himself into a fervor, circling the table Coleman lay on, displaying a psychotic expression, twiddling his fingers together in anticipation and muttering an unending string of gibberish. Every so often, the incoherent rambling was interrupted with an uncontrollable exclamation of rage. His gait and appearance resembled something more similar to Quasi Modo or Gollum. Sometimes he would interlace his fingers on the back of his head as if he were protecting his ears from some unperceivably high pitched bombardment, the whole time an inappropriate smile smeared across his face. His eyes set in deep, dark, sleep deprived sockets.

Bethany sat in a pew near the front also smiling garishly as she squeezed and stroked her breasts to the tips, arousing her rather large, bovine like nipples until they protruded through her polyester blouse, inexplicably without the hindrance of a brazier, moaning in climactic long tones with each drawn out, deliberate stroke.

Smith's ravings were becoming more audible. "Yes! Yes! I have done good for the Lord. His kingdom will prevail. It is come to Earth. My master will arrive soon. (Bark) I can feel his presence. (Growl) It draws closer! (Yip)" As he bounced around, hobbling like something straight out of 'Planet of the Apes'.

The wooden double doors at the entrance opened delicately and a hooded figure in black entered. It was Simon. He was exhilarated. Panting, out of breath as sweat raced down his cheeks, the hood from his loose fitted sweatshirt concealing his eyes, he strode toward the pulpit.

Smith collapsed into prostration, shouting. "Redemption! His Lordship's worshipful beast lives! The miracle persists!"

Bethany matched his supplication by

kneeling toward the aisle, bowing her head as she steadied herself with her forearms on the respective backrests.

Simon calmly slid past Bethany and rose the traditional three steps to the worship area. He remained behind the cotton fabric visor effect of the hood. Coleman could see now, as Simon brought his hand to his mouth to compensate for some indigestion he was experiencing, his maw was smeared with blood.

"Hail to The Great Satan!" He exclaimed, his fists thrown out at 45 degree angles as he stood over the altar.

Smith could scarcely contain his jubilation. He beamed with pride, waiting patiently for acknowledgement. His eyes darted left to right with anticipation.

"Gary. Stop it! This isn't you. Please, let me go. You've been a member for so long. What happened to that Gary? Where is he? Can I talk to him?"

Gary snickered at this, lowered his hands to his hood and finally revealed himself to the church. Bethany clapped to herself enthusiastically and bounced up and down in her seat as though Simon had just unveiled a bulleted power point presentation for ending poverty worldwide.

He addressed Coleman, "My name is Freeney. Gary Simon is dead." He spat with contempt, the blood from his mouth spraying. "He died long ago because your God killed him. And *you* were complicit in the act." He leveled an accusatory finger in Barry's direction.

"That's not true!" Barry countered. "God would never give up on you. He wants you to be happy."

"The musings of a fool." Freeney rebuffed. "Either a fool or the shameless propaganda of a desperate creator. And you are no fool, are you, Pastor Coleman?"

Coleman remained silent with incredulity. His eyes burned with anger at the betrayal by one of his flock. Though he was doing well to contain his rage, he knew his only chance was to appease the maniac to some degree, with his body language at least. But he couldn't quite justify a response to begin with. It was certainly a loaded question. No. He didn't consider himself a fool but his own doubts led him to reflect on all possibilities at all times. There were some things he still struggled with himself. If he was correct about his convictions, then why was there any room to question his perception in the first place? On the other hand, if he were to admit to Gary that he was no a fool, he would, by process of elimination, be in effect admitting shameless concessions, giving Freeney some kind of moral high ground. If he'd been in his right mind, he might easily have been able to argue more effectively but it was difficult to think quickly in the compromising position he now found himself.

Freeney sneered and chuckled at Coleman's inaction. "You're God is a deceiver! If he wouldn't give up on us is immaterial. Why, I contend, would he place us in a juxtaposition to begin with? If he truly cared about his children, he wouldn't let them wander aimlessly into rush hour traffic. Indeed, you need look no further than your own miserable situation to find the answer to your absurd conjecturing. What merciful God would leave you to the wrath of The Great Freeney?" He raised his fist in victory and held it like a boxing champion at the mention of his name.

Bethany let out a feverish orgasm at Freeney's exclamation point. One hand could be seen on the side of her face, bracing herself from the light headedness. Smith, next to the podium in a squatting position, was beating his hands against the ground wildly with approval. Freeney altered his fist to an open palm, bringing the outcry to a halt.

"No. Your God plays an insidious game with our lives as though they are worthless, leaving us in a shroud of ignorance then punishing us with full force when we err. He is a disabler. A tyrant. He demands fealty and hides behind a false promise of inclusion when anything but total submission is unacceptable. He is more a Wizard of Oz than an almighty benefactor. Yes?"

The twisted logic stung Coleman deeply with the realization of the hopelessness in changing Gary's heart dawning on him. He'd given over to the dark side completely.

"You see, Pastor Coleman, in a way, I owe you. Your ineptitude as a leader has funneled me into a land of delights and imagination. I have fallen into the fold of my savior, Lucifer, the bringer of light. The revealer of truth. The most powerful angel and sympathizer of mankind. A freedom fighter and revolutionary in this battle for liberty and the sole voice of reason and advocacy in a sea of fury and ignorance!" His voice rose into a crescendo with every statement.

"No. No. No. No. No. No. No. No. No." Coleman was steadfast in his denial, though he was sickened with Gary's rationale and saddened by the spectacle unfolding. He shook his head with each point Freeney the demon levied.

"Oh, yes, Pastor Coleman. Yee-e-esss." Gary brought his face close to Barry's for emphasis.

Had he been a more rebellious man, he might've spit in his tormentor's face but the thought actually didn't occur to him. Perhaps Freeney thought he would do so or the obnoxious breath and spray of blood and detritus from his maw would further goad his victim into lashing out so he could justify some perverse punishment.

"You see, Barry. Where your God casts us away from his love, Lucifer accepts us. Regardless of our iniquities, all are welcome. All are accepted. If you think about it, our family is most American in nature. Just like radiant Lady Liberty on Ellis Island in all her glory, holding her torch of truth to the heavenly infidels, incinerating them!"

With this he broke into a psychotic laugh. Smith began his ground beating routine while the tawdry Bethany, having strewn her legs over the backrests of the pews, had begun rubbing herself, her dress skirt revealing white nylon panties, letting out a series of violent orgasms as an overture to Freeney's rebuttal. The scene displayed was a sordid, demented madhouse and it was, frankly, far more than Barry's psyche was prepared to handle. He burst into tears as Freeney grinned with satisfaction as though he had brought in a blue ribbon winning sow at the town fair.

"Oh, what's wrong Mr. Goodie Two Shoes? Did reality just creep up and slap you in the face?"

Coleman was too distraught to focus on the line of questioning, though. A part of him must have known what was about to take place. Gary Simon beckoned over to Smith, who predictably obliged. He produced his police issue Taser and placed it in Freeney's hand. He adjusted the knobs on it and pointed the infrared dot onto Barry's chest.

"Don't be afraid of the truth, Pastor Coleman. I know sometimes it can be.....oh, I don't know, shocking? Aaaaha ha ha ha ha ha! Hahahahahahaha!"

Gary activated the 50,000 volt taser into Coleman's chest. The metronomic snap of electricity coursing through the wires with their prongs dug into Barry's flesh beneath his denim dress shirt. Barry couldn't even scream. He was having too much trouble dealing with the jolts that just kept coming without cessation. His face turned red and all the muscles in his neck tensed until his arteries and capillaries threatened to jump out of his skin.

"Really?" Freeney gestured at the hapless Coleman. "This is the so called Guardian of the Book?"

Simon adjusted the tazer for more strength and the rate of electrical synapses complied. As Barry suffered and struggled, naturally Smith continued with his floor beating exercise coupled by a cheerleading movement of waving his fists above his head, still in the crouching position. It was as though he were attending an Aerosmith concert in Mordor.

Bethany was so excited, she began rearing her arm back and bringing her open palm down upon her erogenous zone with full force nearly, it seemed, at the same rate of the taser snaps. Her repeated climactic outbursts echoed throughout the chamber with chilling reverberation.

It seemed as though Freeney was content to dull the battery of the compliance device in this fashion. Barry began gurgling and foaming at the mouth. His elderly frame, though well maintained, was simply unprepared for the trauma it was absorbing this evening. Just when it seemed he was about to succumb to the barrage of voltage being levied upon him, Simon finally depressed the trigger and tossed the device aside petulantly.

In the ensuing silence, Bethany could be heard bringing her hardcore masturbation session to a close. She lay in a heap, her legs and arms thrown over the pews, exhausted from the exertion of the hyperbolic performance.

Freeney took from his cloak, completely unprovoked, a porcelain commode covering. It was perhaps 6 or 7 lbs.

"Now, you pretentious child, I shall squash you like the bug that you are!" He shouted as he brought the commode covering down upon Pastor Coleman's head with such magnitude that he was propelled into the afterlife instantly.

CHAPTER 15

Patrick and Madison convened on the front porch. She'd intelligently flipped the porch light off before sliding out of the front door, though it's creaking seemed deafening to her, as Patrick made his way back out her window and climbed down the sturdy wooden patchwork fence the Henley's had constructed to accommodate the missus' taste for jasmine.

Maddy hadn't the presence of mind, or wardrobe selection maybe, to wear all black. Her bright pink hoodie bounced as they strode through the desolate thoroughfares, presciently avoiding over exposure from street lights when possible. Armed, they were less afraid of the thing as before yet didn't quite grasp the 'acting natural' concept to avoid profiling from any straggling neighborhood watch people or late patrol.

They moved quickly, darting from block to block, slowing their gait to accommodate the odd passing motorist. Patrick switched his phone to silent and instructed Maddy to do the same.

It was almost 1:00am. Patrick was breathing heavily, though they hadn't had a demanding journey to this point. Maddy took note as they were adjusting their phones.

"You ok? Why are you breathing so hard? You're shaking."

He avoided eye contact, exhaling a gust of strife.

"It's just, I really wanna get that thing."

"I know."

She placed a thoughtful hand on his arm. She squeezed his bicep flirtatiously, felt the hard object of the gun handle Patrick had cleverly stowed in his jacket sleeve. He felt her acceptance; felt her encouragement. They naively believed they posed a legitimate threat to the behemoth what had accosted them in the park. They knew the odds were against them but the degree of difficulty they would surely encounter was proving to be elusive. Life was placing an absurd mismatch before them and they were showing their youth.

He was eager to pursue the cause of his angst. He ushered his young accomplice out of the scope of the street lamp, closer to the fence line of the nearby residences and produced the .380 caliber handgun, preparing to storm the park. They had not considered the monster, most likely imbued with heightened senses, could probably see in the dark quite effortlessly. If it were anything relative to a bat as they had originally surmised, then it's advantages would be even more considerable in the nocturnal environment. Whether it was the emotionally charged aspect of the moment, that being vengeance, or the propensity for the youngest of us to mismanage logistics, they intended to ambush the beast unawares by means of sheer quickness.

Once they were within the radius of a few properties adjacent to the park, they broke into a full on sprint as if they were charging a WW1 trench line as they negotiated the iron car barrier at the entrance. At least Patrick resisted the urge to let out a battle cry, though the temptation was present. They charged down the gravel path in a frenzy, nearing the meadow where Rory had made his last stand, scanning the night sky and murky fields for a black mass, anything that might disparately resemble the figure they hunted.

Verily, they must have come to terms with the futility of their attack plan as the granite trail cracked and hissed beneath their tennis shoes, announcing their presence to the wilderness community. With the revelation of their clumsy gaff, they brought their gallop down to a trot and toggled their position closer to the grassy, earthen terrain. Their eyes bulged, not only for the absence of light but, at least for Patrick, the sheer indignation of the self-inflicted wound, foolishness was bringing them onto the battle field.

He brought back the hammer on the Ruger manufactured self-defense mechanism, his finger slipping anxiously, and sighed in relief as, luckily, the hammer hadn't gathered enough inertia to strike the round with the proper conviction needed to ignite the gun powder. He quickly composed himself. *Everything's ok. Hope she didn't notice what just happened.* This time, he used two thumbs and deliberately pulled the hammer back until it clicked into place. Now his senses were on alert and he was relishing the feeling of empowerment.

They crept closer to the clearing. Patrick probed the air in various directions, slowly scanning the horizon with the nozzle of the weapon as Maddy adjusted her position, slightly to the side and aft of her friend, making sure to stay in his zone of protection but not to cross paths with the line of fire. Though the clear night sky hadn't given way to the clouds which had produced sprinkles earlier, the combination of the modern day city light pollution and the sheer strength of the moon's ambience poking through the heavenly veil provided enough visibility for them to make out the landscape of the prairie. Patrick recognized the location where Rory had engaged the creature and snuck closer, like a child in his socks and pajamas tip toeing through the house in hopes of catching Saint Nick during his run.

"Maddy." He murmured, covering his lips in an attempt to downplay the sound. "I'm going to check out the spot. Watch my back." He could sense her nod of compliance.

Despite the lack of stars, the bright purple sky was more than sufficient to uncover the layout of the rough terrain. Patrick stumbled over the footing; pebbles, rocks, large rocks, rich earth, ant mounds, weeds, thorns and clumps of grass. He was confident no one was too close, though he couldn't be sure of what lay hidden beyond the intermittently strewn cirrus streaks. As he traversed a small ridge of vegetation, the sight of Rory's sacrifice came upon them quickly. Patrick and Maddy balked at the discovery of a large concentration of blood soaked soil complimented by Rory's trademark black Chuck Taylor sneakers as well as a formerly white sock.

Patrick's fists clenched with rage and he had to catch himself as he nearly pulled the trigger on the already cocked weapon inadvertently. Maddy burst into tears, though she was careful to muffle her sobs with the sleeve of her hoodie.

"Oh, Patrick." She whimpered. "How could this happen?"

Patrick searched the sky for answers. He wondered the same. God's mercy could be undeniable, yet there seemed to be a willingness to harvest the lives of the young and innocent which always escaped explanation and created a confusion many adults perceptibly shared.

"Something's wrong. That thing's not supposed to be here. We're the humans. We're the rulers of this planet. We're not supposed to be hunted."

Madison sniffed, resisted the urge to wipe her nose on Patrick's sleeve. "I know. What do we do now?"

They'd moved into a crouched huddle now, still maintaining a higher level of alertedness.

"I don't know. That thing could be anywhere. You know what really pisses me off?"

"What?"

"It could be out there, doing that to someone else, right now!"

Madison slugged him on the arm.

"Don't say that!" She chastised in whisper.

"No, it's true. Don't cover for it. Be honest."

Patrick could feel his blood beginning to boil. He could tell the next thing Maddy was going to suggest was they pack it in. But the thought of her, his only ally throughout the trauma they'd experienced, abandoning the task at hand all but pushed him over the edge.

"Come on, you animal!" He was having a meltdown. "Show yourself, coward! It's kid mcnuggets you want? Come and get it! I'm ready for you! You like picking on little kids? Come on!"

Maddy recoiled from his outburst. "No! Stop it! What are you doing?"

She was still speaking in hushed tones. Patrick ignored her pleas.

"I'm right here! What are you waiting for? I'm only fourteen and I'm right here!"

At the saturation of his words, the silence didn't sit well with him. He aimed the barrel of the weapon at the clouds and blasted a round into the night. The thunderbolt echoed off of the trees at the edge of the clearing. Patrick was surprised at how well he handled the kick back from the powerful hand cannon. The rush was exhilarating for the time being but then it began to wane and an emptiness filled him.

"Patrick, you can't do that. We could get in trouble."

Her point was valid. Initially, they'd felt foolish alerting a superior force to their presence. As they waited, they struggled with their feelings. How else were they to summon it? But then, when it became obvious that nothing was responding, there was the failure of the task and guilty relief of avoiding a difficult challenge.

"Nothing's happening, Patty. We need to get out of here."

Patrick searched Maddy's eyes. Please don't tell me our journey was in vain. But it wasn't her fault. You can put yourself in a position to win, that doesn't mean all the variables are going to come together to allow you to seize victory.

"Where do we go? What do we do?" Patrick fretted. "There's nobody. Our parents aren't going to help us. No one believes us. We can't go to the police, especially with this hot gun."

Maddy brainstormed for a moment. "I don't know. You know, in times like these, my dad says you can always turn to God."

After another pause, as her words of wisdom sunk in, a light went off in his head.

He broke the silence, "What about the church? Isn't that the best place to talk to God?"

"I think so, yeah. Aren't they having a lock in tonight? They should all be there, in the gymnasium. Maybe Pastor Coleman can help. We can trust him."

They moved with purpose now. Patrick resisted the urge to walk with the fire arm in clear view. Always a good idea to be prepared but no sense in inviting unwanted attention. He had just discharged a stolen weapon within the boundaries of a municipality on a nationally recognized holiday. Sometimes, the same thing you take for granted as a safety net is the same thing most threatening to you.

Predictably, they hadn't traveled five properties past the park when headlights flashed and exposed them as they emerged onto the thoroughfare. They were caught like unsuspecting deer, frozen in time, their eyes wide with shock.

Maddy was already on edge and couldn't counter the opportunity to run. She broke out onto the sidewalk. Patrick, forever loyal to his friend, reluctantly followed suit, cursing under his breath. If only she could've chosen to return to the park where at least they would have the advantage of unpredictability and a bit of cover. It was a hasty decision, an anxious one. And it would cost them.

They were barely parallel with the vehicle before Patrick noticed the unmistakable blue and red flashing lights of the law man. Maybe Maddy hadn't noticed because she'd kept moving to Patrick's chagrin. But they both knew their evasion was futile when the cop simply pulled the police cruiser directly behind them in one fluid u-turn motion. He didn't need to get on the loud speaker. They knew there was no point in continuing their flee. Though they'd never been on this side of the equation before, they'd witnessed attempts to escape the grips of law enforcement on reality t.v. and it had always ended in favor of the authorities. From the layout of the neighborhood, someone on foot would have little chance at concealment unless they could dart quickly into a backyard. The streets were wide, long, well-lit and packed with houses. The neighborhood association, perhaps intentionally, had sanctioned the excessive use of hedges and bushes, trees. There simply weren't many options for one wishing to elude an automobile on foot.

The kids exchanged worried looks, squinting with frustration. A tall, hefty patrolman emerged from the cruiser gripping his utility belt like John Wayne. The way he sauntered over seemed to scream 'You in a heap o trouble boy'. His waist bulged like some kind of human tuber as he approached the kids, a code relayed to central command through his shoulder radio unit.

"Hey, guys. What's goin on?" The candor was light and harmless.

Patrick answered reluctantly. "Nothing much. I guess you startled her."

"Hmm." The cop considered this, rolling his

kneck side to side. The reaction made Patrick uneasy. It was like he was gearing up for a bar room brawl. "So, that's why you guys ran from me, an officer of the law?"

They glanced at each other from the corner of their eyes. This feels like a trap.

"We didn't know you were police." Maddy reasoned.

The police man cut her off. "It's not that dark out here under the street lights, young lady. Why would you be scared of the police? What do you have to hide?"

The duo didn't quite have the sophistication to manipulate the peace officer the way they may have wanted to. They looked like they'd been caught with their hands in the cookie jar.

"Don't have an answer for that, do you?"

Patrick searched for one but he was hampered with a cotton mouth. This wasn't going very well.

"What's your name, son?"

"Patrick Duffy."

"How old are you?"

"Fourteen."

"Your parents know you're out here? It's too late for someone your age to be out here right now. A lot of young people get involved in mischief on Halloween night. Y'all wouldn't be up to something like that, would you?"

They shook their heads vigorously.

"Patrick, would you mind coming over here

and having a seat in the back of my car?"

"Uh, no sir."

This did not look good. Patrick's optimism interjected, *maybe he's going to take me home like some of my other friends.*

The burly police cop escorted Patrick to the back of the Crown Victoria with his arm in his hand firmly, careful not to grip Patrick too hard. The back passenger door opened with a gesture and he maneuvered Patrick into position between himself, the open door and the seat now exposed to the cool night air. Patrick thought he was about to be seated but not so.

"Ok, now place your hands behind your back for me."

He guided his left hand to the crux of his back while he beckoned for the other one. Patrick was filled with a brief impulse to wiggle free and escape but reason restrained him from making a mistake he couldn't soon erase.

"Wait, I thought you said I was just going to wait here?" He pleaded.

"No, sir. Don't worry. Right now your just being detained."

He coolly grabbed his other hand and placed it into the solid grip of this left hand already holding the other. He reached to the back of his utility belt in a well-rehearsed motion and quickly brought hand cuffs out, latched them onto Patrick's helpless teenage wrists caught in the vice grip of the lawman's mitts.

"But don't I have to do something wrong first?" Patrick tried to find the officer's eyes behind him, searching for some semblance of pity.

"No. This is just for your safety and mine."

"But what did I do?" He begged.

"Why did y'all run from me? That's suspicious activity. Now, do you have any weapons? Any knives? Anything like that? Anything that might poke me? Any needles?"

He'd taken the liberty of running his hands through Patrick's pockets.

"No. No, sir. Nothing like that."

Nothing in my pockets. I just might get away with it.

"See, sir. To be honest, someone had made a call about someone discharging a weapon at the park. They said they saw someone in a pink hoodie, like your friend over there. And-...."

He'd discovered a lump near the elbow of Patrick's beige Polo jacket.

"What's this?" He squeezed and pinched the lump until it formed an outline. "I thought you said you didn't have any weapons."

Patrick remained silent. He had a right to do so. He could also sense the addition of another police cruiser adding it's attendance to the scene.

The gargantuan cop spun Patrick around as if they were dance partners. He gave no resistance. His mind was already wandering to the consequences and searching for any possibilities, however improbable they might be, of salvaging something positive from this situation. Hope wasn't easily visible for Patrick, unbeknownst to him, though the ramifications were potentially serious, his status as a minor would allow for him a much more lenient set of punishments. At the most, he would most likely be absolved of any wrongdoing upon his entrance into adulthood at eighteen years of age. Of course, fourteen was exceptionally young to be considering adult sized penalties as he was.

He felt the massive paws of Officer Mercier, now with blue latex gloves stretched over them, unzipping his coat and forcing themselves down his sleeve. It didn't take him long to locate and retrieve the hand gun.

"Oo! Look what we have here"

He remarked with delight as he carefully laid the evidence on the roof of the cab next to the emergency lights array. His comment carried all the levity of a child emptying his stocking on Christmas day. He clicked on his shoulder unit and casually announced the police jargon.

"Huh. Now, how did I know you were up to no good?"

Patrick didn't dignify a response.

"Go head and watch your head for me, sir. Ok?"

Mercier gently compressed Patrick's body like an accordion into the prisoner hold of the vehicle and shut the door as Corporal Dodd arrived.

"Looks like you got a hot one."

"Yeah, I guess these are the ones runnin around firing shots in the park."

He moved quickly to look as professional as possible in front of his superior, carefully flipping open the cylinder and dumping the shells into his hand.

"Hollow tips, too. I wonder who he stole this from."

"Um, excuse me? Luke, did you say 'these ones'? Where are the others?"

Mercier jerked his head in the direction the teenage girl in the pink hoodie was supposed to be and returned with a bewildered portrayal.

"Aw, crap."

CHAPTER 16

Dawn brought with it the notorious fog which enveloped the tree tops and larger city structures as though someone had unleashed a geographic sized serving of dry ice onto the pine ridge where the township lay. Today's murkiness was coupled with an unusual amount of haze, cutting the visibility even more drastically and coloring the normally purple/grey hue with an uncomfortable shade of orange. Even when the sun had risen to an accommodatable height, it gave the appearance of a 'blood sun' as it poked through the mist just past the treetops at about 8:45 am.

Detective Martin Rosicky was caught off guard once again by the office telephone as he peeled a layer of diced carrots and peas and white onions from his combination fried rice dish from the night before he'd left imprinted on the side of his face and fused to the paperwork before him, having served as his makeshift pillow. It wasn't unusual for him to fall asleep at his desk. Whether it was a convenient excuse for his mother's beguilement or the fact that he was content in his bachelordom, the job seemed to be tailored perfectly to his lifestyle. It also wasn't unusual for him to nurse a flask of Wild Turkey 101 housed in the bottom right desk drawer whenever he stayed late at the office, pondering a particularly uncooperative case.

He still managed to answer the phone in his signature way, though there wasn't much of an audience to appreciate it. What little there was had long been disenchanted with his antics. The morning patrol had already come and gone, debriefing and all. Anyone who might have been put off with his slovenly appearance had long since bumped their heads against the wall in vain attempts to have him written up.

"Good morning." He made a poorly veiled attempt to convey alertness.

"It's Willard again. You up and at em?"

"Of course."

"I've got a homicide for you. In Henry sector."

"Oh, really?"

"Yeah, really. Old lady. Abuela must've really pissed somebody off. It's pretty gory."

"Ok, I'm on my way"

"1604 Tortuga Lane. I've got some coffee here for you."

Fresh coffee from the murder scene? You shouldn't have.

Detective Rosicky pulled the gray Mercury Grand Marquis up to the house on the hill, near the dead end, next to the park on Tortuga Lane to find a hectic display. Upon his emergence from the vehicle, he was made keenly aware of an apparent family member's grief.

A well-muscled Hispanic man with a buzz cut was proving to be a tall order for a couple of officers attempting to provide an added barrier for the yellow police tape x-ing out the open doorway to the abode resting at the conclusion of a decidedly lofty set of steps. The indignation in his eyes and cadence was clear to all.

"So, what? You have me identify my own mother's body and now I have to go away from here? It's my mom! You cops are all the same. Probably had something to do with it! Always covering something up."

It's way too early for this. At least it's not a blank fortune.

Deputy Willard, a tall, slender man with glasses and cropped graying black hair, met him inside the gate at the base of the stairs.

"That's the son." He gestured behind him with his eyes. "He's the one that found the body. We're trying to keep the crime scene as untouched as possible for you. It's not sitting well with him."

Rosicky squeezed his arm in acknowledgement as he made his way toward the steps. This was a touchy situation and no thing for a grunt to handle. As he fought with the nearly vertical stair case, the absence of coffee struck him like a bee sting. He sighed with concession.

"That's why it took you a full hour to get here, cochinos!" He was emitting a spray of saliva into a hapless officer's face that more closely resembled the crash of a tidal wave onto coastal rocks. "Just another dead Mexican in the ghetto, huh? You know there's a cop station not half a mile from here!"

Rosicky inserted his portly, non-threatening demeanor into the fray.

"Mr. Rodriguez, is it?"

He resisted the urge to extend his hand and offer a shake. This isn't a car dealership, someone just wacked his mom. Instead, he brushed aside conventional wisdom and hugged the victim's son. All muscle. Like a Pitbull. Didn't get a hug back. When he released him, he'd expected to see a disarmed look in his eyes. Maybe there was a faint one, hidden deep inside.

"Who the hell are you, the Pillsbury Po Boy?"

Martin deftly sidestepped the jab. He was accustomed to shots at his weight.

"I am Detective Martin Rosicky, Senior Detective, Allenville P.D.."

The officers nearby exchanged looks of skepticism. They knew it to be an embellishment but no one was vying to correct him. Apparently, he was willing to make himself the target of any ensuing criticism, which was a welcome gesture. Rosicky was going to freestyle this one. He'd borrow lines from some movies or books and make up the rest.

"So, you're the one in charge of fucking up the investigation or just burying it in some file cabinet in a basement somewhere."

"No. Nothing like that at all. I know what it's like to be a minority. My family is Polish."

He studied Rodriguez closely. He'd accepted the lie. The vein in the middle of his forehead had begun to dissipate back into his skull. Maybe they had some common ground after all.

"I grew up in the Bronx. Nobody looked out for the little, fat Pollack. My mother was murdered as well. That's why I went into law enforcement. So no one would have to go through life like me, wondering who did this to my mom."

"I'm sorry about that." The air force man was a teddy bear after all.

"Look, I know this is very difficult." He continued. "But I'm going to do my very best to catch whoever did this. In a way, it's almost like I have a chance to avenge my own mom."

Rodriguez looked like he was just about broken. Rosicky had him staring at the ground.

"Well, I'm going to get to work. Every second is precious in the first forty eight hours. If you'll go with Deputy Willard here, he's going to ask you some questions that we need to ask so we can make progress on this. After, if you don't have anyone to stay with here in Allenville, he'll set you up with a hotel room and we'll pay for it."

Rodriguez buried his head in Willard's chest and began bawling as the law man was making an effort to gingerly help him down the stepping stone stair case and away from the crime scene or, as Rosicky privately referred to it at times, the executive boardroom.

Martin Rosicky ducked under the crime scene tape and was greeted by a scenario which could more aptly be described as a cross between Hamburger Hill and Nickelodeon Guts. Surprisingly lonely, the personnel was trying to respect the alien landscape strewn with the strange green goo. *Great, I can even hear my own thoughts in here.*

He struggled with his footing, trying to step around the lakes of Gak. An elderly woman lay face down in a comingled pool of blood and Gak near the kitchen table. A bizarre symbol, like the one he'd seen back in Simon's cell, had been outlined in the pool of Gak.

It could only be described as some kind of masochistic sun. It was a circle, complete with sun rays but it's face had been dissected by an upside down cross, forming a somewhat make shift ball gag. Disconcertingly twisted he thought. The etching had an uncanny way of suggesting the defilement of almost everything sacred to man with but a few strokes. An abomination. Rodriguez's rage could only be empathized with. *God help the poor soul that ever tried to desecrate my mom's house like this!*

The green puddles were littered with indiscriminant paw prints. Typical old lady stuff, he thought. The kitties were nowhere to be seen right now, though. Probably scared off by all the unfamiliar faces. Cats are so secretive and mysterious, he mused. Just like women.

"Her name's Alma Rodriguez, 72." Willard appeared behind him. Martin was startled but he didn't show it. His reaction time was still slowed due to the lingering hangover and lack of caffeine. "We gathered some statements from the neighbors. She stays by herself, just her and her cats. Goes to church and bingo. Other than that, she's known as somewhat of a medicine woman."

"Medicine, eh? Think there could be drugs involved?"

"I don't know. I guess everybody has a different definition of medicine. I know back in high school we sure did."

Rosicky snorted.

"At least we have some finger prints this time."

"Oh yeah?" This fortune cookie had lottery numbers and everything. "Whatcha got?"

"Two sets, on the front and screen door, the doorway wall and the light switch. Youngsters. One we don't know, the other matched some files from June. Rory Sieverson, 14. We got a squad car on the way to his folks' house right now."

"Good." Rosicky remarked as he cupped his hat, ducking under another set of police tape, heading for the exit.

"Where you headed?"

"Oh, you know. Think of me like Toucan Sam.

Sometimes you just gotta 'follow your nose'." Willard completed the sentence with him underwhelmingly.

"You need to eat, my dear."

Mrs. Wilkerson placed a heaping bowl of salmon bisc in front of her eldest daughter. It was replete with Premium saltine crackers stacked in rows threatening to spill over the large dinner plate the soup bowl rested upon. It smelled delicious, with vapor wafting seductively towards Challista's face but she shunned the thought of food and even went to the length of pushing up from the table to seek refuge in the outside world shining through the kitchen window. Isn't it ironic? The most desirable of dishes make themselves available to those who eye food with contempt for whatever drama of the moment that might be taking precedence in the grand center stage of life.

She nervously peered out the window, her eyes much less focused on what lay beyond the glass, her strained sockets, moist with mascara, searching for answers that dared not surface. Her elbow, supporting her head acutely, her back slouching to one side in order to compensate, sat below a fore arm whose respective hand had been converted to handkerchief/chew toy. Her nervous habit of gnawing, grinding her teeth, was honed in on it as the object of an oral fixation that seemingly knew no sate.

"If she won't eat it, I will."

Kathleen Coleman, Challista's full grown daughter, without hesitation slid the platter over to her with eager eyes for the creamy seafood specialty, throwing back her long blonde locks over her shoulder so it might not interfere with the steaming concoction percolating in the ceramic dinnerware before her.

"Let your mother have that, Kathy baby. She hasn't eaten today. Don't you want some, hmm?" Her plea falling on deaf ears.

"Aw, jeez, ma. You and daddy haven't even fought before. You should see me and Devon. If we don't have an argument at least once a week, we start to lose that, you know, fire."

"Kathleen, what have I told you about taking the Lord's name in vain?" Challista snapped. "Your father is a man of the clothe, for crying out loud."

"'Jeez' really isn't the same thing as saying 'Jesus'." She muttered defiantly.

If her mother hadn't been experiencing some hardship, she surely would've made the utterance more readily audible but she stiffened it out of regard.

"Don't tease her right now."

The matriarch comfortably presumed the referee role, whether the circumstances called for it or not. Maybe she fancied the business of her offspring, by proxy, hers. Or perhaps she inherently knew that without arbitration from her position, there was little reason the large family would successfully navigate discrepancies and maintain solidarity. They did, after all, tend to gravitate toward the Wilkerson's home, all four generations now. *If it came from my loins, it's my business. If it happens in my home, it's definitely my business.* The logic, actively considered or not, was sound.

"Do you mean to tell me," something odd struck her, "That you or he actually instigate conflicts between the two of you?" She scowled.

"Yes." After a slight pause, "To be honest, it's usually me. Devon is so non-confrontational and laid back."

"That's awful." Granny shook her head in disapproval.

"Oh, it's better that way, gramma. It's usually over something small so he knows everything's ok. Like the remote or what kind of diet we're trying that month. He can be so passionless. I just love to ruffle his feathers or just nag him until he explodes. It's so worth it."

Doris Wilkerson coyly pretended not to know what her granddaughter meant. Kathleen scooped the thick and chunky preparation with a couple of crackers as makeshift spoons. Any time is a good time for bisc. She wasn't exactly famished but the discomfort of her mother's distraction and resolute resistance to the hot meal made her nervously hungry.

Doris soothed her daughter's anxieties, rubbing her back lightly, trying to gain her eye contact back into the kitchen.

"It's past noon, honey. Let's try to eat something, I'm sure he'll call any moment now."

"The lock-in must have finished up a couple of hours ago. Why hasn't he called or come over already?"

No one seemed eager to address the enormous pink elephant in the room of what the discrepancy between the two of them concerned. They'd quarreled feverishly in the early years of their marriage but once the children were locked into their routines, the little things began to seem insignificant. Barry was quite agreeable and perhaps they were simply a zodiacal powerhouse. Once the church had been created and subsequently built a substantial following, things had really kicked into gear and fallen into place. Amazing how some families can create so much. Businesses, homesteads, multiple generations and yet, the same amount of time passes for some who may have lived just two or three years.

"I want to go. I want my husband."

The public realization ended the chatter in the kitchen. She wants her husband. There's certainly nothing wrong with that. Challista listened carefully for anyone to dispute that assertion. She turned from the window to face the countertop.

"I. Want. To. Go. I. Want. My. Husband." She carefully enunciated each word.

"Ok, I heard you the first time. What do you want me to do about it?"

"Don't take that tone with your mother,

Kathy." Doris objected.

"I want you to take me to the church to check on him. If he's not there, then you can take me home."

That sounded reasonable enough. The short moments of silence acted as little, mini-affirmations.

"Well, ok." The daughter replied finally. "I've already called his phone a couple of times, though. He must be busy with the parents or something."

"What? How long have you tried him?" She demanded. That's my husband we're talking about. I should be mitigating the frequency of communication here.

Kathy's eyes shifted as she recalled. "Like three or four times altogether. I just wanted to check on him. I know you guys are going through something so I just figured he needed some private time, you know? I could never imagine going through a thirty year marriage to Devon without a few vacations from him, maybe even every season. Did you ever think maybe you were suffocating him?"

Challista's eyes glared with rage. She looked like she wanted to say more but she came back to herself. Her daughter was a petulant little brat but she meant well. There was always genuine concern hidden behind her reckless jabs.

She deliberately snatched up her purse and headed for the door, retrieving some sunglasses from inside as she walked briskly. The best bet to

get something done is to not justify unconstruct-
ive comments. She could feel Kathleen's eyes rolling in her skull behind her back but she knew she
wouldn't have to wait long for her daughter to
come outside with the keys. She was still obedient
deep down inside. She'd only developed her re-
sentful sarcasm since starting her own family and
unwittingly mortgaging her free time.

Kathleen joined her mother street side where
the gray Toyota Prius was parked. Still crunching and munching on some saltines, her long coat,
scarf and purse in tow. Challista couldn't fault her
pedestrian attitude. *I didn't exactly tell them what
I've been through in the past twenty four hours.*

They climbed into the hybrid car and situated themselves for the short trip to the next
neighborhood over where the church lay. How
many times have we nonchalantly driven a family
member somewhere relatively close by to satisfy
whatever whim or notion that might be begging
their attention? They'd be traveling for roughly
five minutes but, for Challista, it could never be
fast enough and she knew there was no point trying to rush Kathleen. Didn't mother's always seem
to be in a rush? We always want to honor our
mother's wishes but how are we to know when
times are really critical? *Why worry my daughter if
I'm overreacting? What happened to me was serious
but Barry is all I know.* He'd always been there and
at this point, there was no reason to think otherwise. Except intuition, of course. And that was a

big reason. Not that she had the time or patience to explain it to her eldest daughter. She already knows everything anyway. There was simply no explaining a mother's intuition. Something was wrong. Very wrong. All that remained to be seen was what exactly. This was not good.

Kathleen used a stop sign to light up a Marlboro light 100, perhaps intentionally not rolling her mother's window down for causing such a fuss on an otherwise enjoyable day. She was almost positive whatever dispute they were having was her mom's fault. Besides, it was her window. She can do whatever she wants with it. *Who doesn't smoke these days, anyway? Especially someone from her generation.*

Challista resisted the urge to chide her as she activated the switch, rolling her window down. It would just add precious time to the already torturous trek. Her mind was restless, miles away. Is he ok? Is he alright? Did the lock-in happen? Could he have been so distraught from that awful event that he'd gotten hurt somehow or, God forbid, hurt himself? She guiltily recollected how she'd collapsed in her parent's guest room, exhausted from the ordeal, as soon as she'd heard Barry burn off the night before. She just didn't have the emotional energy left over to monitor the situation overnight like she might have wanted to.

As Kathy navigated the neatly trimmed yards and well maintained roadways composing the makeup of the suburban landscape they inhabited, Challista rummaged through her purse for a particularly evasive pack of Trident, anything to take her mind off the impending confrontation. She finally discovered the spearmint chew as they rounded the corner of the traffic light on May Flower Way, where the Abundant Grace parking lot rested on the right.

The activity in the township was unusually light. They hadn't noticed the quietness and non-existent nature of the normally bustling community. Strangely enough, though there was routinely a small number of various cars and trucks parked at the church for whatever reason, there were a fair amount more than usual greeting them as they pulled into the south parking lot of the Lutheran Church. As the Prius slowed to adjust to the extra objects on the tarmac, settling in on a strategic location, the freshly tenderized piece of Trident gum fell out of Challista's agape mouth nearly back into the paper wrapping from which it had so recently been removed. Was the pressure from all the stress she was experiencing all too much? Because she was most assuredly hallucinating, at least she hoped so.

A fiery spectacle was unfolding before her. She rubbed her eyes in disbelief. Still there. At the far end of the fresh asphalt, from the East parking lot, where the recent additions had been taking place, it was a CAT bulldozer, engulfed in flames, turned the corner of the building and swiveled directly toward them as though attracted to their position by a terror honed magnet.

"Oh, my God!"

They hadn't been travelling faster than five miles per hour up until that time but Kathleen Kennedy slammed on the brakes with conviction. At first, the nature of their concern was less for the loss of property than any humanity that may have been affected by some unfortunate accident. That concern quickly ricocheted back to their own wellbeing as, inexplicably, the emblazoned construction vehicle actually appeared to pick up speed towards them. Columns of fire shot out from all sides of the cabin and even from beneath. The fireball seemed to rise and fall with intensity as though the carnage was alive with some sort of combustible respiration. It very much resembled a modern day fire breathing dragon.

Kathleen braced her hands against the steering wheel. Her first instinct was to stamp down on the accelerator and speed around the behemoth but the way the newer cars had chosen to align themselves in their respective parking spaces, she was effectively hemmed in to a corridor of mayhem as the bulldozer appeared to be gaining momentum in their direction.

Challista was panicking. By now they had surmised that they were in some real, immediate danger. The urge to unbuckle her seat belt and bolt from the steel death trap ran through Mrs. Coleman's mind but a few points stayed her hand. Logically, she might actually be in much more

harm if she abandoned the safety of the Prius'
coat of armor. Furthermore, what kind of mother
would she be if she selfishly abandoned her first
born for the benefit of her own safety, even given
the inherencies of this logic defying phenomenon.
There was no way someone could be alive in that
machine, operating the controls, steering it. Yet it
moved with purpose, intelligence.

Her hand, the pack of gum squeezed tightly
with duress, convulsed with urgency as she hesi-
tated to give direction or even scream for some
kind of stupification at her daughter's inaction.
With time running out so quickly, do I risk dis-
orienting her with a command when a split second could easily be the deciding factor? Why do I
even have to consider whether or not to tell her to
get us the hell out of here? Isn't she supposed to be
an alert driver or something?

She finally cut through her barrier of indecision and shouted a command at Kathleen, her
voice rife with alarm. She could see Kathleen
had locked up. Without time to prepare one's
self mentally, it is difficult to gage just how long
it may take for your mind to adjust to an unpredictable or implausible event until it jumps
out in front of you, much less how you might
react. She'd had her foot firmly on the accelerator
far too long. The chaos ensuing had preempted
even their awareness of it until now. They hadn't
moved because her other foot remained absent
mindedly planted on the brake pedal, sandwiched

to the ground beneath her gray, aqua and yellow Asics running shoes. The smoke from the burning rubber and horrible tire screeching noise, no competition for the abominable sight of the dozer, not to mention the wretched twisting metal sound accompanying it.

"Put it in reverse and back out!" She yelled hysterically.

Kathleen's motor skills must have been want for commands because she readily complied with her mother's instruction, perhaps too quickly. No sooner had she shifted into reverse, her all too sudden release of the brake pedal caused the Prius to slingshot uncontrollably from the unanticipated power of the already rapidly spinning tires, catapulting them erratically into a white Chevy Suburban. There they rested for lack of orientation. If Kathy had been more resourceful, she might have been able to throw the hybrid back into 'reverse' and salvage a makeshift escape but the subsequent confusion was taxing them extra moments they no longer had the luxury of utilizing.

The bulldozer slammed into them headlong, pinning them to the Suburban, it's scoop wedged conveniently beneath. The possessed machine wasted no time lifting the plate roughly 8 feet high, capsizing the unmatched Toyota Prius with it's passengers screaming in terror.

This time, Challista's indecisiveness was nowhere to be found. Now that her door was furthest from the maniacal contraption, she forced it open and managed to free herself from the seatbelt, allowing her to plop herself down to the earth where she scurried to some nearby vegetation.

Her daughter wasn't as fortunate. The plate lifted to it's maximum height and the dozer's mammoth wheels crushed through the cabin like an ordinary twelve ounce aluminum can of beer at a frat party. Kathleen was buried beneath the massive rubber and torn violently under the traction as it ploughed through the Prius with little resistance like a tank on the battlefield.

CHAPTER 17

The grimy, thick Allenville smog oozed through the streets, winding and wrapping it's way around the buildings of the commercial sector of the township. The overcast skies had prevented the escape of the colloquial mist Allenville was famous for as brunch time approached the part of the city known as "The Drag". This was the area designated to distract the local community college students from becoming too visible to the municipality's more tourist driven historical district and town square. It was an intimate, two square mile collection of pubs, night clubs, restaurants, tattoo shops and novelty stores. If there was some place where someone might wish to indulge in activities of an illicit nature, they would invariably be directed here.

The Drag was home to a rag tag group of street urchins known affectionately as the "Drag Dogs". Primarily composed of college drop outs who'd moved to the city and used up all of daddy's good graces as well as his dime, effectively stranding themselves. Others, more migratory, having trickled in from various parts of the country, the Drag Dogs had established themselves as part of the environment. By closely observing patrol routines, they'd developed some effective techniques for inhabiting their territory. With nothing more than a wrist watch, some could stagger their sleeping patterns for certain areas at certain times, thus avoiding detection. The presence of numerous alleys didn't hurt either. Others simply forwent sleep altogether for days at a time with the assistance of a cocktail of street drugs they'd purchase with pan handling proceeds. If they reached a point when their bodies could no longer continue without sleep, some would flop at a bus stop or alcove and rely on the generosity of law enforcement to turn a blind eye. City council had long ago approved statutes effectively outlawing homelessness.

This sector of town is precisely where Detective Martin Rosicky found himself. He'd ditched the all too recognizable, unmarked Grand Marquis in the adjacent neighborhood and was walking briskly, his hands pocketed in the retro throwback trench coat, the brim of his fedora pulled low over his brow, obscuring his face, avoiding eye contact. Not only was this the typical time that the junkies began getting restless and searching for passersby they could ask for spare change but Rosicky was doing his best not to be identified by any members of the underworld. He was a lifer in the Allenville Police force and there were only so many trouble makers in the small town. It wouldn't take much for a rapscallion to catch a glimpse of his face and recall him from some previous encounter.

Martin rounded the corner of the Chinese restaurant he'd ordered from the night before which was ironic in and of itself because 'Wok in the Park' had essentially cornered the market for Asian cuisine delivery in Allenville. The turn took him to a more unglamorous offshoot of the Drag and 'Wok in the Park' had adjusted it's business appropriately. Away from the eyes of it's clientele entering through the front, a nondescript side door served as a go between for their delivery boys who'd lined the curbs with their bicycles and high miles per gallon cars. Above this door was Rosicky's destination. A fire escape stairway had been unrolled to street level, leading to an otherwise forgettable second story loft. Any party with enough free time to devote a fleeting thought about it would probably have reached the conclusion it had some connection to the establishment below. A tiny accounting office, someone's kids secondary apartment maybe, a crash spot for immigrant kitchen workers who could save money and send back home to their respective families but this couldn't be further from the truth. The one window displaying a wall of tin foil wrapped insulation could easily be written off as an attempt to save money but anyone with a rudimentary familiarity with paranoia might know better.

Rosicky furtively checked his vectors and, once satisfied, scurried up the fire escape and onto the little ledge just outside the unremarkable second story door, even bearing the same coat of paint as the rest of the building on that side.

Some minor commotion in the alleyway stayed him momentarily from signaling his arrival with his knuckles. A gang member had demanded and then received the wallet of a passerby not 20 yards below his position. *Well, nothing I can do about that from up here,* he scoffed. *Except, I have a badge. And I have a gun. But I've got bigger fish to fry. I'm not about to risk making my best informant for the sake of some schmuck's credit cards he was either too ignorant or too cowardly to protect.*

Distractions aside, he tapped out the agreed upon knock sequence and waited. Out of the corner of the window, he regarded the lens of a closed circuit camera. The red light indicating it was recording. And he would expect nothing less. Martin could hear latches being disengaged from behind the door. Soon, it was poked open just enough to allow the detective to gain access and he was ushered into the one bedroom apartment with great haste.

"C'mon, hurry up! Get in here." The voice whispered with a noted degree of irritability.

Rosicky was now face to face with Diego "The Nose" Marscese. They called him that because he had a large one. More closely resembling the beak of a toucan than anything else and he had the propensity to stroke it methodically when pensive. "The nose knows" he always used to say when confronted. Marscese shut the door behind him and activated a series of bolt locks.

"Can't you dress like a normal person for once? I can't have people thinking I just talk to the police willie nillie like it's normal or something."

Rosicky was taken aback. He gave himself a once over.

"What. I think I look like a perfectly reasonable scumbag."

"Of course you're a scumbag. You're a cop."

"In this trench coat, I could easily pass as your average, run of the mill pervert." Martin retorted.

"Nobody dresses like that anymore. You look like a pervert scumbag cop."

Rosicky smiled to himself. The two had an 'Odd Couple' like dynamic that allowed them to communicate unfiltered.

Little was known about Marscese's background. Rumor had it a stint in the Navy, some even contended he was at one point a SEAL, had landed him a field position in the CIA where he'd served a tour in the Middle East. The Nose had developed a system of information gathering which benefitted from word of mouth reports on the ground as well as a conveniently placed group of associates in various industry and academia positions he could call upon at a moment's notice. Detective Rosicky'd stumbled upon his operation by following a trail of bread crumbs through the underworld and quickly assessed that it would be worth the professional risk to allocate some "black funds" and place The Nose on payroll. It had proven to be a rather effective gamble. At this point in the game, Martin reasoned that Marscese could effortlessly have relocated seamlessly once he was discovered or, worse, wouldn't have had to over exert himself to simply make the detective "go away". But they'd nurtured a symbiotic arrangement as well as a veiled amount of respect for one another.

"Cigarette?"

Martin declined the pack of Marlboro reds he'd been offered. Marscese cleared away a slew of papers and dirty laundry which was oddly situated in the living room and made a seat for himself. It always amazed him how an ex-military man could live amongst such disorganization but then again, there's no telling the type of transformation one's mind might undergo after years and years of chaotic business arrangements, unenviable romantic soirees, troublesome flashbacks of combat scenarios gone awry. And yet, who's to say the appearance of a disorderly livelihood was just that and not strategically perpetuated?

He was tall and robust. His attire reflected the clutter. A Syracuse Orangemen t-shirt, basketball shorts, flip flops. Rosicky knew he had a gun nearby or on his person but he couldn't tell where. With The Nose, anything was possible. He wouldn't be surprised if there was a gunman lying in wait in the bedroom should something unexpected transpire. Marscese popped open an exceptionally crafted laptop on the dining room table that had been placed next to the mattress where he slept. A veritable Pacific Union style procession of modems, routers and other gadgets led to a well-used power strip. Rosicky had no doubt Marscese's equipment was state of the art, virtually unhackable and not to be found on the shelf of a Best Buy.

"I don't know how you do it." Martin quipped as he situated himself in the canvas lawn chair, not exactly a beacon of light in the world of comfort. "You know, get such good results in this pig pen."

"Let me remind you how this works. You ask questions; I give you answers, simple as that. Besides, you should be the expert in pigs and pig lifestyles."

Martin shuddered at the comparison to swine. The wisecrack had clearly hit a soft spot. He spoke up, trying not to let it show.

"Tell me about one Gary Simon. I think he murdered an old lady in the ghetto."

Marscese ignored the question. Instead, reached over the table to a stack of olive drab dossiers and procured one. He calmly unwound the string from the doily cinching it closed, opened it and, shielding its contents from Martin's curious gaze, shuffled through the leaflets and large print polaroids.

"Oh, yes. The hospital escapee." The Nose commented nonchalantly.

It bothered Rosicky to no end how Marscese already knew details about a confidential ongoing investigation, a fresh one at that, but The Nose payed him no mind. Casually, he shut the folder and tossed it back on the desk with the others as if it were a poorly conceived middle school book report. Next he leaned back into a makeshift back rest composed of dirty laundry and propped a foot across his knee. Marscese began stroking his gargantuan nose the way he was known to do.

Martin wanted to stand up and slap him in his pretentious face. What is the God damn hold up? But he wasn't about to be the first one to break the silence, thus tipping his hand. A sort of impromptu 'quiet game' ensued. *Is this the part where I'm supposed to toss him a brown paper bag with bundles of cash in it? I hope not. Because last time I checked, The Nose had been paid in full, handsomely at that.* One would think he could afford the rhinoplasty many times over by now.

Marscese brought his hand down from his nose and grabbed a zippo from the nightstand. He lit a cigarette and inhaled deeply on the tobacco. Smokers have such a way of building the suspense. It was wholly unfair. The Nose eventually replied, smoke wafting from his nostrils as he did.

"Simon is unimportant."

Rosicky sighed. "That's not exactly the answer I was looking for."

"If you don't like it, you can take a flying fuck and a rolling doughnut. Which, for you, might qualify as meals on wheels." He shot back.

"Tuh." Martin scoffed.

Another cop joke. *I could've watched Law and Order for that.* This was useless. Martin placed his hands on his knees, bracing himself to get up. Then Diego "The Nose" Marscese piped up.

"I can, however, inform you on good account that someone is attempting to open a gateway to hell at the Lutheran church. Go there. You will find all the answers you are looking for."

As Patrick regained consciousness, he became painfully aware that he was the victim of an overtly cruel headache. He'd never partaken in any libations but this, he surmised, is what the dreaded hangover must be all about. As the blur melded into a semblance of reality, he also pieced together that his environment was a bit more confining than what he was accustomed.

Of course!

Last night. I got arrested.

The events came back to him slowly, followed by more painful realizations.

I hope Maddy's ok.

Apparently she'd quite resourcefully seized the unforeseen opportunity that had materialized when Patrick's arresting officer made his unfortunate discovery of the haphazardly concealed firearm.

But did I squeal on Maddy?

No.

I wouldn't have.

He surprised himself actually in his resolve. When the cop's supervisor had arrived on scene, he'd questioned him, albeit without reading him his Miranda rights, rigorously about his "lady friend" as he called her. There was even a hollow threat made, citing a Patriot Act clause, in which the authorities would be permitted to imprison him for up to ninety days without even telling his parents, in an effort to entice him to spill the beans about where he'd acquired that pistol and what the identity of his partner in crime was. All they had to do, he claimed, was deem him to be an "enemy combatant". But Patrick knew he was bluffing. He'd regurgitated that hogwash assuming that Patrick would be petrified by the language and too young to press the issue should the legality of saying such a thing come into play. Perhaps all those crime scene investigation shows he'd sat around watching with his folks after dinner were finally paying off.

Either way, he was well aware that, whether his crime was justified or not, these cops were no good. They were up to something and they oozed sinister. It was more than enough for him to concede that they couldn't be trusted, especially with Maddy's whereabouts and identity, which would do nothing anyway but lead them to the original owner of the weapon. Whenever someone was guilty on t.v., they usually refused to answer questions without the presence of their lawyer and that had been enough to back them off for the time being.

Patrick hopped off of his plastic mattress and gaged his surroundings. Fluorescent lighting. Institutional, off white paint. Concrete with steel shavings mixed in it to make it extra consistent. The lack of anything remarkably visual alone was enough to dilute one's outlook. The whole thing was wantonly devoid of stimulus.

He hopped back onto his bed and stood on it, peering out of the window slice he'd been afforded, hoping to find some refuge in the outside scenery.

O, how he longed to be outside of those walls. Anywhere in his field of vision would do, even if he were to randomly materialize in the middle of that thoroughfare during rush hour traffic.

Wait.

Was that......Madison? In the distance. Meandering through the adjacent pasture. Or was his mind just seeing what it so desperately desired to see?

He refused to entertain the idea that he had let her down. He had to find a way to get to her. To *help* her. He'd already lost one friend, he wasn't about to lose anoth- Oh, poor Rory! His heart hadn't had time to grieve the loss of his best friend to the beast. His world was seemingly collapsing all around him and it was an awful lot for a young man of his age to be confronted with. But in many ways, perhaps he was more prepared to take on these hardships than many full grown adults under the same circumstances. Though many might wrestle with the prospect of epic tragedy and world crushing events on a daily basis, by that very token, the realization that at least something of that nature will occur as an eventuality could easily contribute to a palpable level of panic and instability. By contrast, someone Patrick's age may not be aware of what they could potentially be missing in the future as well as a lack of regrets concerning the past, they might not know that they should be panicking. Is it not strange that so many fear death and, not simply the potential act of dying but the conceivable passage to the next experience, even though it is as normal as birth itself?

Yet, how could this have happened?

Twenty four hours ago, he was your average, all-American Joe enjoying his high school time with his friends. Now, he'd been a witness to the gruesome execution of his closest colleague at the hands of a nightmarish monster. He'd stumbled upon the murder scene of a gentle, elderly woman, watched as his other friend was subjected to scrutiny, been arrested at a young age for a potentially serious charge, all the while facing obstacles as the lone voice of sanity without a hint of support or guidance from the adult community. And there was nothing he could do about it from his present confines! He slammed his fist against the bullet proof, 4" thick glass in frustration.

Patrick's mind raced with possible scenarios. He had to be missing something! It just wasn't adding up. He's only fourteen for God sakes! *How can they justify holding me here in adult jail? Don't they have to notify my parents?* Of course, even if he could get ahold of them right now, would he really want to? Only a child can truly appreciate the wrath of a furious disciplinarian.

Patrick twirled around. He could feel that creepy sensation of being watched by less than innocuous eyes. And, sure enough, much to his chagrin, he could see, in the lower portion of his observation window facing out into the cold, drab hallway, a grim face gawking back at him. The visual was most unsettling for his young mind. *Oh, my God. How long has he been there watching me?* More disturbing, perhaps, in that his antagonist wasn't saying anything. Just peering at him behind deep, dark, sunken peepers and a putrid, emaciated face. The voyeur had the look of one who'd been marching through the Mojave for a week without food or drink and Patrick had taken on the appearance of a Cornish game hen.

Patrick could feel the adrenaline surge with the revelation of the silent and ominous threat. He fought the temptation to run up to the door and yell, "What do you want?" But thought better of it. What if his action merely provoked the peeping Tom to come into his quaint abode? Though the freak was clearly pejorative in stature, his ghoulish demeanor was enough to convince Patrick that he didn't want to find out what that guy was capable of. Now that he'd had a bit more time to assess the spectacle before him, it could be seen that the figure opposite of the partition was looking at him so intently that he was fogging up the window and actual sputum and nasal debris was accumulating on the glass closest to his olfactory senses.

Patrick wisely chose to stay in the standing position on top of his bunk. If that creep did find a way to get in, at least he would be occupying the high ground. Presently, the boy was trying to summon the courage to be proactive and take the initiative in the uncomfortable exchange his tormentor seemed content to perpetuate. The best he could think would be to ask a harmless question, possibly humanize the ambiance.

"Uh, hi."

No response.

"Have you seen a guard around here? I'm starving. When do they serve lunch?" he ventured, trying not to sound too vulnerable.

The minion's expression slowly evolved into a smirk. After an awkward pause, he answered with unadulterated peculiarity. His voice had all the likeness of a goblin or Gollum like creature.

"Oh, how ironic! Don't worry, little boy. We'll all be eating soon enough."

The Quasi Modo-esque henchman began

chortling and snickering, spittle and oral detritus splattered indiscriminately on the observation window glass, fogging it up. The uneasiness magnifying exponentially, to Patrick's bemusement, as the fiend's chest heaved up and down more and more with each obnoxious guffaw, he could now make out the appearance of a shiny badge and sheriff's uniform. Apparently they really were just hiring anybody these days.

"Can I make a phone call?" Patrick interjected, if only to break up the jail guard's inappropriately long episode of self-amusement.

"What?" He replied, taken aback.

The weirdo blinked at Patrick, wide eyed as though the funny spell had been instantly shattered.

"Yeah, I never got a phone call. I get one free phone call, don't I?"

He'd actually gathered this from the movie "The Matrix" starring Keanu Reeves. Patrick wasn't totally convinced this was even true and reluctant to decide if he would be calling his parents or anyone else in particular should he be given the chance to do so but it seemed to have an immediate effect on the mad man's annoying little demeanor.

There was no laughter coming from the other side of the partition now as the freak regarded Patrick with contempt. It finally breathed a sigh of concession, "I'll go and fetch the supervisor for you."

Well, that was easy. Patrick hadn't entertained any ideas that his request would be received with even a grain of consideration. Why would an organization of hooligans with little interest in decency, not to mention rule of law, give credence to such a claim? But in the meantime, it appeared to take this aspect of Patrick's due process quite seriously, strangely enough.

Of course, now the prospect of dealing with that twisted soul's higher up was making it's presence known and he was beginning to wonder if his little maneuver was about to blow up in his face. Anyone who was willing to approve of the type of employees Patrick had been exposed to surely couldn't be up for eagle scout honors. He was about to begin the process of psychologically recovering from his probable wrong footing and hyping himself up for another confrontation with inanity but for an intense, inescapable light permeating through the room, blinding him. This light was accompanied by a trance like, high pitched intonation which modulated at various points and carried with it the characteristics of a tuning fork.

When his eyes were finally permitted to adjust, he could discern that the powerful light was originating from a single tennis ball sized point, hovering in the very center of the cell, about three and half feet above the ground. Patrick tried to control his astonishment. Was this some strange new form of experimental interrogation?

Now the ball of light began to grow in size. As it enlarged, the irradiant glow it produced, brightening the surrounding walls, was decreasing respectively. The ball of light appeared to be absorbing the incandescence from the ground and redirecting it into it's evolving shape. Ultimately, the anomaly took on the appearance of a man. He was elderly but well preserved. Despite his balding head and thick white beard, his skin conveyed an impression of health and vitality, especially with the expression of warmth and kindness the man's Caribbean Sea blue eyes instilled. He was dressed venerably in a vintage cotton suit and dress shirt. The color scheme was composed of a variety of golds as the patterns of light green, yellows, browns and whites blended tastefully. As the details of the old man's appearance revealed themselves, Patrick kept waiting for his feet to take their place on the ground. But they never did. Instead, his image bobbed in place and wavered up and down in the center of the room, a halo of bronze encompassing him.

"Do not be afraid, Patrick. My name is Giovanni Bernard and you have been chosen." Giovanni's piercing blue eyes bore into his consciousness.

He squinted, trying to maintain focus on his paranormal messenger.

"What do you want me to do?"

"What I want and what you want are one in the same." He said this whilst spreading wide his open palms as if his words themselves were revelation. "When you are ready, you may begin."

The visage floated away from Patrick now, toward the cell door and seamlessly, as if through some kind of spectral osmosis, melded into the door, emerging out onto the other side. Giovanni gave Patrick a wink and then his image continued slowly gliding down the corridor and out of sight.

Patrick blinked in amazement. It could hardly be considered extreme given the sequence of events he'd been privy to in recent times but still, none the less, he wondered if what he'd seen had really transpired or was he beginning to crack? Is this what people with schizophrenia experience when their minds have been exposed to inordinate amounts of pressure? Maybe his mind was conjuring things that were more or less agreeable in order to compensate for the inexplicable occurrences he'd witnessed in reality.

Patrick bounded off of his bunk and across the 6' x 9' cell to the door and, leaning against it, strained his neck, adjusting the angle, trying to manage a glimpse of where his celestial visitor had vanished to. He'd toggled for the position that would allow to see the furthest down the hallway and there wasn't a trace of Mr. Bernard. Verily, the negligible amount of inertia exerted from Patrick's adolescent frame he was absent mindedly applying to the door was just enough to deactivate the latch. It popped loudly as the steel portal lurched past the mechanical bolt. Apparently, his door had never been properly secured in the first place!

The action startled Patrick, his mind simply wasn't expecting the door to be so easily perforated. For a brief moment, the notion had occurred to him that, as his hands were now occupying a space that was far beyond where he had taken for granted that they could possibly exceed, that perhaps he was truly ignorant as to the extent of his own strength.

Am I really bursting through this wall like the Kool Aid man?

This tidbit of unanticipation wasn't all that unwelcome but it brought with it a new set of dilemmas. Was I not just wishing for an opportunity like this? It surely seemed too good to be true. Patrick was compelled with a significant urge to dash through the threshold and make a break for it but a bit of logic caused his hesitation. What if he got caught? Wasn't he in enough trouble as it is? That could possibly add to the amount of time he would be jammed up. Then again, it wasn't as if he could get into much more trouble at this point. Especially with a bunch of crazed heathens at the helm, what difference did it make? Perspective prevailed as the realization that there must be countless individuals at this moment in time who would relish the opportunity which had miraculously fallen in his lap. There's no telling what some would be willing to trade for a bite at the apple that even somewhat resembled what he'd so freely been given. And he didn't even sell his soul.

Patrick threw caution to the wind as he brazenly pushed the metal door open and slid out into the chilly labyrinth. Whatever they might do to him out here could be no worse than what they likely had in store for him in his cell, he reasoned. Except here, at least, he wasn't trapped like a rat.

He latched the door shut behind him and instantly felt vulnerable. A rapid glance in either direction of the corridor confirmed that he was indeed alone but the presence of security cameras interspersed every so often meant it was a certainty he would not stay that way for long. He quickly came to the conclusion that time was of the essence. He began moving in the same direction he'd seen Giovanni disappear moments earlier, lightly pattering the balls of his feet against the glossy institutional flooring.

His progress was short lived though, as his fears materialized rather abruptly in the form of a mammoth, rotund jail guard with a buzz cut emerging from around the corner of the elbow at the end of the passage way. Naturally, he was followed by the simian gait of the first guard he'd encountered previously when he'd inquired about his phone call. Patrick could see now that the lower ranked corrections officer was probably of a more normal stature at one time but his spinal structure had been severely distorted by some means giving him the exaggeratingly pejorative height he now assumed.

The boy froze like a deer caught in the headlights. He was busted and there was no getting around it. They would descend upon him like a coordinated assault by a pride of lions on a lame zebra in the Serengeti plains. Patrick braced himself for lift off. His best weapon would be agility. There was no way his underdeveloped frame would do any measurable damage to their bulky adult vessels but he might be able to out maneuver them! Besides, they didn't exactly exude the insinuation of dexterity. Just what was it about jail guards and police men in general? Was there some unwritten requirement that they be overweight? It says here; you're 5'11", 175lbs. Sorry, not fat enough. Put on another 75lbs and re-apply. Probably something to do with all that coffee and pastries he concluded.

It was a tangent he didn't quite have time to explore but as he'd been able to mull it over, he couldn't help but notice the lawmen weren't barking commands as he might've expected there to be a degree of consternation regarding his disposition outside of his cell. Nor had they taken any measures to alert the rest of the facility or apprehend him and they weren't all that far away from him either. The heavy set one was lumbering toward him in typical fashion. If they had seen him, they were doing a damn good job of concealing it. Actually, Patrick felt quite confident now, there was no way that they couldn't see him. But apparently they didn't because if he hadn't so deftly sidestepped them, the big guy would've walked right over him.

As mysterious as it might be, there was no time to do a synopsis on what exactly had transpired here. He didn't wait for them to make it to his cell and freak out when they realized he wasn't in it. He scurried down the hallway in the direction from which they had come, navigated through the rest of the catacombs composing the central booking facility, avoiding eye contact with staff as much as possible and, unceremoniously, walked out of the front doors, completely unobstructed and unnoticed.

CHAPTER 18

Meanwhile, at Abundant Grace, Freeney had been overseeing a series of renovations. Above the majestic pipe organ towering over the altar area, the picturesque stained glass display overlooking the pews featuring a rendition of The Messiah clad in a red robe had been obscenely vandalized. A pair of devil horns and Van Dyke style moustache with soul patch had been crudely painted on in jet black. The unpalatable artist had even seen fit to add an extra line protruding from The Savior's mouth, replete with squiggly line meandering up, indicating a lit cigarette or joint maybe. There was even a cartoon dialogue bubble next to his head with a quotation from none other than Porky the Pig with his most infamous of dismissals: "That's all, folks!" A plethora of candelabras had been instituted throughout the perimeter of the sanctuary, lending to a more Romanesque environment as a small army of imps had now insinuated themselves amongst the assembly of twisted humanoids who'd since gathered. The men and women in attendance, based on their garb, could be seen mostly to represent an assortment of public service positions, law enforcement composing the overwhelming majority of this cross section. Lawyers, medical workers and other high profile government positions were counted as well as some of the more pedestrian members of society. There were even a handful of McDonald's employees present as the scene more closely resembled a pit of vipers in terms of the mannerisms and body language the group had acquired as they mingled and interacted.

One of the imps, in an act of shameless self-indulgence, had arranged a group of soccer moms including Mrs. Bethany Simpson, seemingly intoxicated from a voluminous combination of box wine and prescription pain pills and clad in all manner of inappropriate evening wear such as lingerie and leather bondage outfits with crotch less undergarments, in a kneeling semi-circle before him as they took turns fellating his reptilian phallus with vigorous aplomb.

Near the back of the pews was a man who somewhat bore the resemblance of a cross between Pinhead and Ghostrider. As he sat with a slovenly affect, his feet nestled on the back rest before him and his elbows spread across the pews he occupied, the fire from his needle ridden head raged with an eerie, supernatural calm. Maybe by divine specification or perhaps some other phenomenon, the flame seemed to possess an innate virtue of exclusivity in that it did not seem to be in danger of igniting the mahogany or what would seem to be the highly flammable embroidery of the pew itself. Presumably the result of a voodoo experiment gone bad, one could only conjecture as to what he had done in his past life in order to earn himself a position among this tawdry coalition of iniquity but no one could be sure. In fact, it was one of Satan's selling points. While transparency and openness served as some of the basic cornerstones of God's Kingdom, Lucifer stressed the value of privacy among his constituents. While new arrivals to Heaven might be shocked to discover old acquaintances or family members they'd long since written off, their celestial merit was easily accounted for and none were unwilling to be made known their heroism and integrity. All good deeds would come to light in the Holy Community. In contrast, whatever unsavory transactions had taken place between an individual and The Devil remained private and without directly confronting said persona, one could only be left to wonder about the conditions of their allegiance.

The vulgarities taking place within the sanctuary chamber were compounded by the heinous atmosphere perpetuated by a duo of imps in the far corner, who'd nursed a campfire sized blaze fueled by a stockpile of Bibles and hymnals, bulletins. As they monitored and tailored it's growth, the disturbing mood created was that of an unsightly, grimy mist that left soot caked on the walls and windows as ashes and scraps of light, airy Bible tissue fluttered to the ceiling and drifted down in a macabre, dismal type of snow. If this wasn't revolting enough, the grotesque hell spawns had seen fit to construct a makeshift spit suspended above the embers as sparks and juts of flame snatched at the rather substantial rat carcasses having been skewered and slow roasting. Freeney had expressed exceptional pleasure at this. Commending them, "It is indeed right and just that we return to the ancient ways of the burnt offerings and create aromas which are pleasing to the Lord." The stench from the damp, matted hydes of the rodents was absolutely hideous and the campfire steward imps cantankerously tinkered with and adjusted the level of incineration the pest corpses absorbed as they smoked, rotisserie style over the hot coals.

Now Freeney, the man formerly known as Gary Simon, climbed the podium to address his wicked cohorts. He removed the hood of his signature Russell Athletic sweatshirt to reveal a crimson splotch, the remnants of whatever foul cuisine he'd been gorging upon, painted across his maw sloppily. He spread wide his arms, fists clenched, forming a 'Y' symbol in exhortation.

"Ladies and gentlemen," He announced. "May I have your attention please? Excuse me."

But his incitation had fallen on deaf ears. Nobody was paying attention. The mob was too engrossed in their respective immoral activities.

Freeney grew frustrated. "Shut the fuck up!" He yelled indignantly.

The crowd froze as though the needle had been lifted from a record. They quickly became aware of their dispositions, recalibrating their attention to the pulpit where Freeney, the alpha male, was to orate. The chamber was silent. Only the slurps and smacks of the latest soccer mom to offer her oral services to the sex crazed imp's scaly obelisk, presumably too focused on her task at hand to be distracted, could be heard. Freeney continued undeterred.

"Hail Satan." He decreed.

The throng replied in unison. "Hail Satan."

"My friends," He slowly brought his hands to rest on the sides of the podium, his eyes bulging with demonic adrenaline. "It is with great pride that this installment of the Order of the Silent Sun shall commence. I, Freeney, shall preside as honorary chairman."

He had their full attention. They'd filed into their respective pews forming a sort of obscene congregation. Enhanced by his speech, their heads bobbed and nodded along with approval at the nuances of his enunciation.

"To begin, I want to congratulate all of you for making the journey to this fine assembly. As we all know, it is not always easy to stand up for liberty, especially when you are encompassed on all sides by a sea of oppression. Many of you are no stranger to the concepts I speak of. Yea, it is difficult when the Creator has set us up for failure from the beginning. It is a truly twisted contention of reality to subject one's own children to an unattainable standard and heap unwarranted and ruthless punishment upon them when they fall woefully short of those unattainable goals. The Deceiver claims to offer us unconditional love and so called "free will" and then reprimands us for utilizing it. It is not love to desire slaves. We are sentient beings who prefer something better in life. And we deserve it!"

Freeney punctuated his viewpoints by slapping the podium with an open palm. His audience was thoroughly encapsulated, hanging on to his every word.

"But luckily for us, our fearless leader, Lucifer, rescued us at our darkest of hours. He demonstrated to us what true love really means when he offered us acceptance, regardless of what pleasure we partake in, regardless of what "crimes" we've been accused of."

With each argument Freeney successfully raised, his comrades in debauchery grew more confident and excited. They began working themselves into a fervor in their accustomed styles of celebration. The men hooted and hollered, galloping about in simian fashion as though they were attending a Rolling Stones concert on Planet of the Apes. They applauded intermittently with bizarre clasps made over their heads as though they were some kind of demented chimpanzees. The others crouched in a squatting position and slapped their hands on the floor with intensity.

The ladies of course, demonstrated their elation with impromptu masturbation sessions, their guilt free climaxes seemingly exaggerated sonically for effect. The imps controlled their fanfare more effectively. They'd doubtless witnessed more impressive spectacles back in the depths of Hades. One, however, was so overwhelmed with stimulation that he actually produced a letter opener and drove it into a peer's eye socket with all the grace of a wielded ice pick. A handful of onlookers jeered and egged him on as he pounced on the writhing victim's circumstance and proceeded to bludgeon him in the face multiple times to the joy of the spectators.

"My friends,"

Freeney liked to address his audience as though he were John McCain before the U.S. Senate floor. He hushed them by gesturing with his hands in a calming motion. He'd whipped them into quite a frenzy but he was demonstrating a high level of control now. He was building a reputation as a gifted speaker.

"Brothers and sisters, far too long have we hidden in the shadows whilst the enemy who is legion ignorantly gallivants and parades in their opulence in a land they, themselves admit they have no right to. That's right, even in their own farcical literature, they patronizingly refer to as "The Bible" as if they are the supreme guardians of truth, it clearly states that this world belongs to The Devil."

Freeney paused for effect.

"Why, then, must we operate in secrecy when we are the undisputed, rightful inheritors of this realm? That is not freedom, my friends. That is not America. That is not truth."

"Here, here!"

"Aye!"

Came the shouts of agreement along with the obligatory 'Hail Satan's.

"You see, my compatriot freedom fighters," Freeney continued. "Our Luciferean doctrines are patently American in nature and precisely that which our forefathers intended. This nation was founded upon the liberty of the individual, something The Believers know nothing about! I say unto you: we refuse to mortgage our identity for a false iteration of happiness! It is even cleverly concealed in our worshipful master's very name. The name Lucifer comes from the combination of two Latin words: Lux, meaning light; and Cifer, meaning carrier or bringer. Just as The Great Deceiver would have us exist on a foundation of lies as he so attempted in the Garden of Eden, our serpentine Lord seeks to liberate us with none other than the truth. While Zeus' acceptance is contingent upon a strict adherence to his outlandish company policies, Mephisto always has room for you in his ever growing family, regardless of your beliefs or actions."

Freeney paused for a moment to let what he was saying seep into the collective consciousness.

Even he was impressed with the ingenuity of his dark overlord's stratagem for recruitment.

"The American Revolutionaries were well aware of this as evidenced by the Statue of Liberty herself in all her glory. Does she ever find it in herself to turn away anyone from the promised land at Ellis Island, hmm? No. As she stands firm and resolute, a beacon of justice in an otherwise naïve world, with her glorious crown of horns, her book of reason and her torch of righteousness she so appropriately lifts towards the cowards in Heaven, incinerating them!"

The nefarious congregation cheered and applauded as though he had just unveiled a power point presentation for ending world hunger.

"But, my friends, I, Freeney, champion of the voiceless, do not stand before you today with mere words. I bring you results!"

With this, he motioned to three teams of imps standing by to his right, left and aft. The grotesque gathering watched in awe as Simon's minions tugged and pulled on tightly woven ropes which could now be seen to have been looped through individual locations throughout the rafters, forming a pulley system. Their efforts revealed the mutilated body of Pastor Barry Coleman, bound by each wrist and tied by the ankles. They raised him feet first to a point prominently displayed above and behind Freeney's head, ultimately obscuring the defaced image of the Lord Jesus Christ. Coleman's dress shirt was hanging over his head due to gravity, revealing an upside cross which had been gruesomely etched into his skin along with the numbers 6-1-1. A hush came over the throng of hooligans as they absorbed the spectacle before them.

Freeney was quick to fill the silence with more propaganda. He gestured at the carcass with an open palm. "This, here, is the steward of this very house of iniquity we now occupy. He'd named it Abundant Grace. Where is your abundance now? Where is your grace, goody two shoes?" He openly mocked the deceased Coleman.

"This man would have us relegated to obscurity while he and his little playmates revel in the fruits of plenty, which was to be OUR birthright!"

Lost in translation was Freeney's attempt to gain interactive responses from his audience but, realizing their obliviousness, he redirected his criticism to the uninhabited vessel which once housed Pastor Barry Coleman.

"Does your arrogance know no bounds, hmm? Even our mere presence in your institution is undeniable proof of the viability of our claims. For what kind of benevolent God would knowingly leave you to the devices of the Great Freeney's wrath?" Freeney capped off his unchallenged volley with a bevy of pelvic thrusts. "Booyah! Booyah!"

The mob could scarcely contain themselves, they erupted with jubilation. Gary was taking the liberty of recycling many of his points to the larger audience but he was growing skilled at driving home his theses.

Simon continued his tirade. "O, what's the matter?" He further mocked his nemesis. "Cat got your tongue? Well, if you don't want to contribute to the discussion, that's fine. But if you're not too busy, we were hoping you'd stick around with us as our special guest. That's right, we certainly don't mind if you......hang around!"

Freeney burst into an uncalled for laughing fit at this feeble attempt at humor. The crowd loved it. His popularity was soaring to dizzying heights.

"But wait! Wait, I'm not done yet." Simon tried desperately to calm himself down, he was clutching at his heart. "I've yet another surprise for you, my brethren in enlightenment."

He nodded at a duo of imps standing at attention next to the large wooden altar table. The ceremonial cloth which naturally overlaid the tabletop was long enough to drape down to the floor. Freeney's underlings carefully lifted it off of the ground and folded it over the top to reveal a makeshift prison cell with iron bars cruelly bolted, containing a disheveled Challista Coleman. She at least had been afforded the dignity of remaining fully clothed, however, so limited was the space in which she was confined that she was forced to stand on her hands and knees like a dog. Her make up ran down her face freely as she sobbed and wept, struggling to digest the horrid scenario she faced.

"That's right. It's the meddlesome encroacher's wife, on all fours like the bitch that she is. And get this, not twenty four hours ago, I did violate her and she participated willingly! Aahahahahahaha! What's the matter? Choir boy not exactly ringing the ol' church bells at home, I take it? Ooh, ooh. Don't look now, lover girl, but I think he's got a better chance of reaching them from his current position. Aahahahaha! So don't say I never did you any favors, you miserable whore!"

Challista burst into hysterics at the terrible psychological beat down she was suffering. She was completely bankrupt mentally and emotionally.

"That's two. Two gifts I bring you!" Freeney glowered like a tasteless Sesame Street count. "Double your pleasure! Double your fun!"

With this he devolved into an end zone celebration style, Macarena inspired exclamation point. The congregation responded in like, resuming their unsavory activities with renewed vigor.

The festivities were cut short however, when the wooden double doors at the entrance were swung open dramatically and a posse of hellions made their way down the main aisle toward the worship area. They were all singing triumphantly and chanting, "Hail Satan!" and "U-S-A! U-S-A!"

A senior leadership imp made his way to the forefront, shoving and pushing his way through the mass with great urgency. In his claws, he clutched a beautifully embroidered, leather bound, ancient, sacred book which he presented to Freeney. The imp leader beamed like a Labrador who'd retrieved a man sized duck from the marshes during a hunting expedition.

Freeney regarded this with awesome severity as it shimmered and glowed in his hands. He was lost for a moment in his thoughts as he examined the artifact.

When he came to, the imp leader was wrapping up his testimonial about it's recovery.

"And you'll never believe where it was." He concluded. "At the adult bookstore!"

CHAPTER 19

Maddy returned to consciousness in her own bed, rays of a soon to be setting sun shining through her bedroom window. She'd cried herself to sleep for the second time in a row earlier that morning and now sleep had become the enemy. The breakfast table had harbored an anxious set of parents and she'd made the decision upon arrival to simply tell them whatever they wanted to hear. It didn't solve any of her real world problems but it would at least buy her time and give her a safe zone with which to build out from. She'd solicited the narrative that she'd succumbed to the peer pressure of a joint or something, 'she couldn't remember which', and that was the cause of all the confusion. In the end, she didn't have much choice. If she'd stuck to her original story, the truth, they would've branded her as a liar. Now she was just being 'rebellious'. Who knows what consequences they could've come up with given the responsibility of her younger brother's well being tossed into the mix for consideration. Are so many eldest siblings unwittingly made into examples? She could be sent to a boarding school, maybe even a mental institution.

The Henley's weren't happy about it but she could tell her father at least was relieved internally to know he was right and everything was perfectly explainable. She'd thrown him a bone, bolstering his perception of reality, which subconsciously might have been all he really wanted to begin with. At the very least, in her mind, she may just be able to salvage a bit of normalcy for her little brother's upbringing, seeing as how her's was already a distant memory, she was beginning to concede.

Then again, what favors would she truly be doing for Jimmy by hiding her head in the sand? Especially with that thing out there. It had come for him, she recalled, and if it weren't for Rory, it would have been him.

Ultimately, her lie was nothing more than a stall tactic and she knew it. But now that the dream world, with all it's pleasantries and attractions, had been used up, there would be more stalling to do because she did not know how to fix things. Patrick would, though. And his loss was weighing heavily now. Whatever she was going to do, however, she had better come up with something quick because as soon as daddy finds out that gun is missing, she will almost certainly become the main suspect.

Madison Henley pulled the comforter over her eyes hoping everything would just go away. Predictably, her doldrums were interrupted by a tapping noise coming from her window.

What now? She was tempted to ignore it. The last time something interfered with her slumber, she'd been treated to a vision of her schoolmate's mangled carcass murmuring her name from beneath her own mattress. But when she reluctantly flipped the covers off of her eyes, she couldn't be more relieved to see Patrick's hapless face peering in from the other side of the bedroom window pane. She leapt off of her mattress like a child on Christmas morning and rushed over to the window. What is this; some twisted episode of 'Clarissa Explains It All'? Maddy unlatched the slide locks with unadulterated glee and drug her friend in by the collar of his shirt. He awkwardly collapsed into a pile at her feet. It wasn't the most graceful of entrances but she could care less. Her one friend whom she could count on, her one true ally and none more sympathetic to her struggle had made a miraculous return.

"Patrick!" She exclaimed in a hushed voice.

"You can see me?" Patrick was struggling to compose himself.

"Of course, I can see you, silly. How are you here right now?"

"I think I have powers."

He coolly sidestepped the question and she wasn't going to pry much further, sensing it was a long winded story. She had what she wanted from the equation and one ought not to look a gift horse in the mouth.

Maddy was so appreciative of his re-emergence, she seized him by the shoulders and planted a firm kiss on his unsuspecting mouth. For all the jovial teasing and prodding he'd imparted on Rory, it was Patrick's turn to display a beet red boyish blush, revealing his age. Madison covered her mouth as she giggled flirtatiously. Patrick wanted nothing more than to explore the sensations of the young infatuation more carefully but the threat of being swallowed up by the ever vengeful legal system loomed large over the both of them. This was no time for celebration. No, the problems couldn't delay being faced and Patrick's remarkable maturity which belied his age would once again surface. Besides, without a solution to all this drama, there would be no enjoying the rewards of life for any substantial period of time and they were both aware of this.

"Oh, Madison. I didn't know you cared." Patrick beamed as he wiggled his eyebrows comically.

"Shut up!" Playfully slapping his arm.

"Listen, toots. I'd love to stick around n' smooch with yas all day but we really gotta figure something out."

"I know. What are we going to do?"

"I still think our best bet is Pastor Coleman. If he doesn't know what to do to help us, no one does."

They weren't the most comforting of words. So far, adult assistance had proven to be a formidable opponent. But at least now they had each other and things were looking brighter. You just can't put a price on the unwavering support of a camaraderie forged by fire.

"Well, I guess we can rule out getting that pistol back." Maddy quipped.

"No kidding."

"Church is far, though. How are we going to get there?" But no sooner had she uttered the words then it dawned on her. A light bulb had clicked on over her head and it was a bright one. "Unless....." She trailed off as the possibilities marched out in a procession through her mind's eye.

"What?"

"Why don't we just take it?"

"Take what?"

"The car."

"Which one? That one?"

"Yeah. Why not?"

It was a duly pointed question. Why not? And certainly, at this point, there could be little argument against it. They were desperate and they were fresh out of meaningful bridges to worry about burning. Put someone's back against a wall and never be surprised at what they could be capable of.

"Let's just take it, Patrick." Maddy reasoned. "It's not like we can get in any more trouble than we're already are in, anyway. If it doesn't work out with Pastor Coleman, we can just drive. We can just get out of here and start over. Move to a different state. It might be hard at first but at least we'd have each other."

The logic was riddled with flaws but that was last on Patrick's young brain. It was naively sweet none the less. Patrick searched her dark brown eyes for any sign of doubt and there was none.

"Ok, how is this going to work? Do I go out the window and sneak back around out front and wait for you?"

"Can you drive?"

"Yes. I think so."

"OK, come on. Let's get moving. But you gotta be real quiet."

"Oh, don't worry. I will be." Patrick gave a look of gross understatement.

Maddy cracked open her bedroom door and peered out into the hallway, checking both directions.

"Ok, coast's clear. Let's go." She whispered.

Patrick followed close behind, mindful he was entering hostile territory once again. Long gone was the convenient advantage of stealth he'd been afforded back at the precinct. Luckily the floor on the second story was carpeted and the staircase, though it was endowed with several demanding, tight turns, was no more than a couple of yards from Madison's bedroom door. The duo crept carefully and were fairly proficient at sneaking as some teenagers are, if they aren't overly clumsy. Of course, no amount of caution could prevent certain household noises from occurring due to the shifting of weight and subsequent drafts transferring from various chambers. Other than that, they'd made it down the majority of the intimate staircase, which was now curling around to the main foyer of the household, without incident before Maddy was forced to make an abrupt halt.

It was Bruiser, the family Pomeranian. She was staring up at Maddy, her tongue hanging in anticipation from a signature oblivious, stupid expression. Unfortunately, the timing of their daring escape was coinciding with Bruiser's hopes for playtime. Maddy was mortified. She was well aware of the pup's vocal capabilities.

"Not now, princess. We're busy. Go away now."

Maddy directed the adorable doggy, gesturing with her finger to 'go over there'. This, of course, only served to further excite the varmint as it predictably confused her instruction with an invitation to play. It yipped gleefully, hopping up and down, yearning to get a piece of whatever it was concealed in her hand. Maddy deftly snatched up the critter, nestling it's snout in the crux of her arm like a baby, muffling the air splitting voice.

"Shh. Shush." She cajoled.

It finally got the message and relaxed, distracted by the avalanche of attention.

Maddy breathed a sigh of relief. She turned her head around to check on her friend and that's where her eye caught a glimpse of someone standing at the top of the staircase, in the little miniature hallway area connecting the bedrooms and overlooking the main foyer. It was big Bob Henley, nonplussed as one might imagine, a look of disturbance and confusion causing his facial features to scrunch up like a crumpled brown paper bag.

"Maddy, what's going on out here? What...."

His focus fell timely on young Patrick, the identified threat to the wellbeing of the middle aged man's household.

"Hey! What are you doing here? I thought I told you never to come back here!" Bob's eyes were flaring with the type of rage that puts the fear of God in men. Never challenge a man in his own home. Especially involving his family. Especially involving 'daddy's little angel'. And especially don't get caught!

The jig was up.

Maddy plopped the fluffy animal onto the linoleum flooring surface as though it were a burlap sack known to house scorpions. *Thanks a lot, mutt*! It skittered across the ground, claws scratching and tapping wildly as it adjusted, barking at all the hysteria.

Maddy slung herself around the banister at the bottom of the staircase and angled toward the doorway to the garage, located in the modest corridor separating the foyer from the kitchen. Luckily, the car keys hung seductively on a hook directly across from the door so one could effortlessly grab them on their way to the car port. And this was precisely what she did in one fluid motion as she bumped open the garage door with her hip. She could sense Patrick closely behind in tow. The giant had caught Jack red handed. Mr. Henley hadn't particularly been known for his violent temperament but, then again, Maddy couldn't recall a more furious expression of betrayal on her father's face before. She was a good girl and the main culprit who was interfering with that was right there, brazenly sneaking about in his own home. The chutzpah!

The young couple propelled themselves through the laundry room doorway and into the garage which housed the silver 2007 Suburu hatchback, replete with overhead bike rack. There wasn't a moment to spare. Patrick slammed the door behind him, anything to buy them a bit of extra ground, as Maddy clicked the Suburu open with the press of a button on the remote key ring. The family vehicle sprung to life with a flicker of yellow and white flashes. They were in their respective seats in no time and Madison was mindful to lock the doors as a priority as soon as they were.

No sooner had she done this than Bob's formidable mitts slammed onto the windshield, demanding their attention. They were followed in rapid succession by Mr. Henley's bewildered, desperate features. His pleas could easily be heard on the other side of the plexi-glass.

"Maddy, don't let him do this. Open the door, honey. Let daddy in!"

Never underestimate the power of denial. As it would appear, Mr. Henley wasn't quite ready to accept his eldest daughter's participation in the trickery. She didn't dare justify the old man by giving him her eye contact. Instead, she responded by sliding the key into the ignition for young Patrick and twisting the automobile into action. A plethora of knobs and sensors sprang into existence, decorating the cabin with a symphony of lights and bells.

"No! No, don't do this! Stop this right now!"

Bob began slapping the windshield with more intensity now, hoping against hope that his eldest daughter would come to her senses. Patrick actually feared Mr. Henley's hand might damage the integrity of the windshield, with such ferocity was he banging upon the threshold.

THUD

THUD

THUD

Madison was rife with poise. She calmly reached over Patrick's head and activated the garage door clicker, sending the suburban portcullis automating upward, whirring at a burdened yet steady clip. At this, Bob disappeared from view. Patrick assumed he had bounded through the laundry room door, where another garage door clicker was traditionally located but enough time lapsed for him to determine that the old man had returned back into the house. He balked at the inference he might be on his way to the bedroom to recover his firearm and the subsequent outrage that would be added once it was discovered to be missing. He could only imagine the different scenarios of ramifications this would give birth to.

The garage door was nearly adjusted to the point where they could fashion an ejection of the automobile from bay. Though precious little time had surpassed to this point, Bob had already made a return, this time with a menacing 9 iron in hand. He began waylaying into Patrick's driver side window with righteous indignation. Within one strike, the glass barrier separating him from the enraged papa bear was totally compromised, sending fragments cascading onto Patrick and Maddy's lap. Patrick shifted his weight all the way to the side towards his friend, anything to escape the onslaught. In this moment, his instincts persuaded him to stamp his foot firmly down onto the gas pedal lurching them out of the garage like a rocket ship launching onto the driveway and quickly down the cul de sac.

Once the Subaru had plummeted down onto the asphalt, he poked his head up and smoothly guided the vehicle out of the cul de sac but not before Bob's golf club clanged innocuously off of the backside of the hatchback, having been hurled from the driveway by the angry dad.

The next few blocks, a veritable tour of Main Street, was an adrenaline fueled blur of unanticipated elation. The escapees may not have actually considered that they would have achieved this level of success and their souls savored the moment in silence.

Once this temporary interlude of triumph had subsided, they found themselves cruising comfortably through a suburban landscape. Patrick had merely been trying to put as much distance between them and the riled hornet's nest that was the Henley homestead but this had probably been adequately achieved a fair distance ago as the thoroughfares became more frequented and thus larger. His lack of hours at the helm of the craft would soon become apparent as a four way stop would prove to be a considerable demand. His primary objective being a desirable speed to create separation, he hadn't fully grasped the concept of the gradual decrease of velocity needed to safely negotiate the octagonal stop sign. More aptly, the fact that they were travelling uncharacteristically fast for a vehicle in that area was lost on them as well. Most likely, they were thinking ahead towards their next objective and the mandatory stop had become more of a formality as Patrick had no more time to all but tap the brakes as he glided through the intersection, prompting the heavy handed horn of a perturbed motorist they'd managed to cutoff in the process.

Madison, though truthfully uncalled for as the honking had returned his focus to the roadway, had sprung to the steering wheel as though

Patrick were unconscious, wiggling it in a plea to gain Patrick's concentration.

"What are you doing?" She scolded. "I thought you said you knew how to drive. You're going to get us killed!"

"No, no." He reassured her. "It's ok. I got it." He was revisiting a more manageable clip.

"Damnit."

Patrick swore to himself underneath his breath. *How many times can one be saved by grace?* He mused. Surely there would reach a point when his luck would run out. The absence of Maddy's criticism was painfully clear now as he turned his head to check the wellbeing of his friend but she was ghost white, her gaze focused solely on a single point in the rear view mirror.

Please, not this. Don't tell me.

Verily, Patrick's lack luster driving skills had realized the one thing they needed most to avoid as his senses calibrated to the red and blue flashing lights rebounding from the reflective surface of the mirror directly into his corneas, settling on a location deep with his spirit reserved only for certain terror.

Patrick shrank with despair. The end to their hopes of escape seemed inevitable now and he felt foolish for allowing himself to think otherwise. He aimed a glance at his young flame. She was still frozen with fright and helplessness. Would this be the last time he would see her? He'd already conceded the grim reality of a difficult life ahead for himself but now her fate was hopelessly entangled with his and the guilt sunk it's fangs deeper into his nervous system, savoring the sweet nectar of defeat.

He allowed the resolve to exit his body and drift away capriciously. Angling the station wagon to the shoulder, there was no more evasion to be had. The jig was up. Whether it was Big Bob having successfully called in their little heist and the station wagon easily identified or his erratic maneuvering had attracted the squad car's attention, it mattered not. The Subaru would not be able to contend a high speed chase with the supedup law enforcement Impala. There was nothing left to do but simply accept the variation of reality in which the good guy doesn't win. Patrick winced at the prospect of frittering away access to whatever dimension existed where they hadn't gotten pulled over and emerged from their harrowing trial unscathed. Jealousy filled him.

Patrick brought the ramshackle bucket of bolts to a halt and shifted the transmission to P. It was all over now. Just relax and let Johnny Law take it from here. Maybe he would make an attempt to contact Maddy whenever he got out of juvie after he turned eighteen. Of course, by then she'd probably have her college picked out and an engagement ring from a promising and capable, young beaux.

Without looking, he could sense his colleague's disgust. She was face down in her lap, hiding behind a lattice of clasped fingers. Reluctantly, his vision returned to the rear view mirror. The driver's side door of the APD Impala had swung open and out had emerged a remarkably porcine law enforcement official. Even though he was still in shock and only halfway paying attention, something struck him as peculiar. If this officer was responding to a grand theft auto call, procedure would dictate that he wait for back up. His course of action was a clear indication that this officer was approaching the situation as a routine traffic stop. It didn't much make any difference to the outcome of course, as it would soon be determined that a crime had taken place and the end result would be the same. But as Patrick's eye drew in more and more detail, he became increasingly aware of a multitude of troubling incongruences.

He could see clearly now, a figure strapped into the passenger seat, it's wings hardly contained by the seat belt, a glowing pair of ruby red eyes betraying it's location, sitting so patiently as if it were perfectly normal, what appeared to be some kind of reptilian creature. If this revelation wasn't strange enough, he could actually make out a set of instructions being relayed to the cop as he hunched over onto the driver's seat to take in his orders and continue to carry out a communique. Patrick could only imagine what was being discussed. Suffice to say, there may have been a great deal or perhaps the hypnotic control the imp was exercising over the law man required so much effort.

It was in this window of time, just before the fat boy began waddling toward the station wagon, that Patrick's breaking point was reached. *Nothing good can come from this*, he told himself. If his treatment at Central Booking had been any indication of what might be waiting for him, the redundancy of a return trip loomed. Foolish it may have seemed, originally, to have attempted escape then, even more foolish now, it occurred to him, to stay.

Madison returned her presence to the cabin of the hatchback with the jerk of the gear shifter into the R position. Her eyes bulged with alarm. She reflexedly opened her mouth to make her protest known but she couldn't bring herself to enunciate it, not once they'd made eye contact. It was a look of resolve she's been eager to see but until this point had not. Without words, the conclusion was totally understood between the two of them. Sometimes life twists and contorts itself in ways that are seemingly acrobatic in nature in order to force one's hand. Despite all of the training and schooling and mindful advice, there really are no written rules and for everyone, at least once, a day comes when the sun doesn't rise. This was one such time and these two adolescent cohorts were well aware of it. You can run from your problems all you want but eventually they'll find you. The only direction to travel reasonably is.....forward.

With that, Patrick depressed the brakes in

tandem with his other foot crushing down on the accelerator. His timing couldn't have been any better. Despite his inexperience behind the wheel, he was able to coordinate the machine to pivot and thrust directly into the police officer, caught in no man's land halfway between the station wagon and squad car. He couldn't have been more caught off guard. The rear bumper of the Subaru slammed into his shins, removing his feet from under him. Of course, the upper portion of the family car was soon to follow, the inertia hurling the large man just far enough into the roadway for the ill-timed arrival of a Ford F-150 pick-up truck to complete the patrol officer's life, with the unforgiving tire of the cumbersome transport reducing his capital into so much apple sauce.

"Oh, my gosh!" Maddy gasped. Her hands speedily finding the sides of her face with panic.

She knew full well the police man's status as an antagonist, a representative of evil. Still, the dramatic conclusion of that life and the sheer gravity of their disposition was not lost on her.

CHAPTER 20

Rosicky found himself in a long, dank corridor leading him from the activity area to what he assumed would be the sanctuary of Abundant Grace. It had been many years since he'd entered a place of worship on his own volition and he was well aware of the irony in that he had come fully prepared to 'break in' as it were, though he had encountered little resistance to his infiltration of the church facility. One can embark on any number of avenues in a quest for knowledge but invariably is led back to an institution of religion. It doesn't seem to completely satiate the unanswered questions left by science and sociology but for thousands of years it has served as a pervasive theme even the brightest can't seem to discount or avoid.

There could be no doubt now. Marscese's information was accurate as always because there was no ambivalence in Martin's mind that this was the epicenter of the maelstrom having enveloped his city.

He had successfully navigated the obstacle course of carnage consuming the parking lot.

Mangled cars, trucks and even heavy commercial machinery, for some reason, had reached a catastrophic end on these grounds. Even the grass itself, normally golf course like by description, in many places appeared to be singed. Despite the light misting of drizzle as a constant in the present atmospheric conditions, whatever had previously transpired must have been quite violent as smoke and small contained fires snapped and popped intermittently. But even the casual passerby would be forced to conclude that something supernatural was taking place here. An ominous thunderhead was forming over the location. Inexplicably, it even seemed to be developing directly from the church itself, one might conclude.

The town was replete with crimes of all types both petty and largescale. Suffice to say, law enforcement manpower was being stretched thinly and at this, Rosicky was not dismayed. He preferred to work alone and seldom called for back up until he had a concrete case built to his liking. The town was, by all accounts, unraveling by the minute but for Rosicky, he found it strangely liberating. He was free to follow his whims without the threat of oversight and it felt like it was garnering tangible results.

He'd arrived with a mindset of negotiating the church house's perimeter by any means but to his perplexity, he'd found all the doors to be unsecured. For such gravitas, the lack of security occurred to him to be a bit lop sided. It was almost as if the phenomena inside was inviting him in.

But now, in the hallway, he was confronted with a measurable degree of angst. Was it really down to him to unhinge the Pandora's Box of mystery? Whatever was going on here maintained all the allure of a dead dog removal from beneath a double wide on a hot summer's day yet still he pressed on. The senior law man crept forward, placing toe before heel so as to stifle the echo of his footsteps in the baron tunnel. The make of the polished granite surface inciting him to control his breathing pattern, he could hear a pin drop from the other side if he wanted to. He was uncannily sneaky.

He was about halfway down the length of the passage now. His mind's eye perceived the supply closet door slightly ajar as he overtook it. Had it been a less precarious set of circumstances, he most likely would've checked it but his eyes demanded their focus ahead. Scanning for movement, he gripped the Glock 9 mm with silencer attachment he'd purchased under the table from Marscese years before. Rosicky was a ghost who could not afford detection and certainly not by any hostiles should his presence be deemed unwelcome. It was a brave new world and the rules were being rewritten in real time.

No sooner had he progressed past the supply closet did the door fling open and Rosicky was made aware that he was no longer alone. He produced his firearm and about-faced, his index finger flexing. Only a minute exertion of pressure would activate the firing pin but an unsettling sight awaited him, prompting his hesitation.

It was a creature, reptilian in nature, on it's hind legs, standing no more than waist high. Martin didn't feel imminently threatened by it's physical stature but for a ghastly hissing noise it emitted, lunging forward at Martin with outrage in it's purple, other worldly reticles.

Rosicky's instincts, as a default, were to err on the side of caution which, in this case, amounted to his trigger finger decisively squeezing off a round, striking the animal squarely in it's chest. It catapulted backward, grunting and squealing with indignation, a bull frog like noise.

The detective took a moment to gather himself. *What the hell is that?* Something that should only exist in a J.R.R. Tolkein book he thought. An organism unlike he had ever encountered before. He could see now, a humanoid figure possessing all the qualities of a snake or lizard perhaps. Moist, scaly flesh. Talons. Fangs. Sparsely situated patches of hair. No, this was not some twisted derivation of an extreme drug addict nor a freak mutation from the animal kingdom. Could this be the infamous Chupacabra? Great, a discovery of National Geographic prestige and his first gut reaction was to murder the animal. His mind parsed through the consequential scenarios, to him the most probable of which involved; odd ball detective, possibly under the influence of alcohol on the job, poaches a federally protected endangered species. 'He's now serving 15 years in a federal prison while his superiors soak up the lime light and revel in the accolades of a ground breaking scientific discovery.'

I am not here right now. This never happened, he reminded himself. Chaos carries with it a convenient little facilitation for the clandestine. He could probably get away with it, no questions asked, with any luck. *I wonder if there are any more of these things out here?* If so, a documented instance of someone getting bitten could serve as vindication enough but he wasn't in a hurry for it to come to that.

He rapidly checked his vectors. No one else had made their presence known, he discerned, and he intended to keep it that way. A devious arch to his eye brows, the only indication he knew he was getting away with something, tampering with evidence. Cops break the law just like everyone else does, a noteworthy dichotomy in the mind of those charged with upholding the law yet also not constrained by it.

Martin moved decisively now. Reaching in the breast pocket of his beige trench coat, he slapped on some royal blue colored latex gloves and located the shell casing having pinged onto the well-polished granite surface where it had rolled teasingly to the crevice where the narrow hallway wall began, shoved it in the opposite breast pocket. Another one or two furtive glances just to make sure the coast was clear.

A filthy, unpleasant, black substance was collecting beneath the 'Chupacabra'. This, he surmised, was it's blood. The animal struck him as wholly other worldly. His first instinct was to drag the carcass back into the supply closet. With any luck, there would be a mop bucket and some bleach or something he could revisit once more urgent matters had been addressed.

Despite it's decidedly lithe frame, it was found to be remarkably cumbersome to maneuver, no less so from the revelation that it was endowed with a neatly folded set of bat like wings. Rosicky wondered briefly if they were strictly ornamental in nature as he could not imagine them creating enough lift to afford the creature airborne ascension, given the mass of the beast in comparison with the size and estimated strength of it's wings. But it wasn't pertinent. This was a hideous, chimera like amalgam. *Is this where my tax dollars have been going?* Surely the product of some off the books, underground military laboratory gone unsupervised.

He had hardly advanced to the threshold of the supply closet with the corpse before he was made aware of the impending approach of others. The echoes of voices and footsteps, and this did cause him duress, incited him to, rather ungracefully, heave the scaly varmint into the abyss, a clattering of various tools and objects followed. He saw no more attractive option but to join his new found, slithery friend in the musty enclave. Perhaps he could learn something from these fresh entrants but he wanted to control that dynamic. The party would be upon his position soon. He left just enough separation between the door so as to have an optimal vantage point to see but not be seen. Gripping his service weapon tightly, he braced himself for the next moment and monitored his breathing.

He could determine there to be two tangos based on the cadence of their footsteps and the light candor they were exchanging. Mortals. It was both refreshing yet circumspect. They were moving briskly, fast enough to justify any hopes that they might overlook the sludgy mess he'd left behind. But Martin had other plans. As soon as the figures emerged past his hiding place, he knew he had the jump on them. He wanted answers and he wanted them now.

Detective Rosicky erupted out of the supply closet brandishing his trusty service pistol. Training his weapon on the unsuspecting passersby, he let out a declaration that had been bottled up for far too long.

"My name is Detective Martin Rosicky and I demand to know what the hell is going on here!"

He subsequently gulped and eased down his sights when it was revealed that the ambushees were just some kids, high school age maybe. They were far less terrified than they should've been, he noted. It was almost as if Martin were a welcome sight. They made no attempt to flee. The boy and girl were exchanging glances of skepticism. Did they doubt that he was an officer of the law? Did he, in his progressed stage of life, no longer convey an air of authority? Suffice to say, these younglings were far too casual in countenance for his liking but yet, they still made no indication of flight. Surely, if they were up to no good, they would display more prominent signs of unease. They merely eyed Rosicky, meticulously scouring for detail. It was as though they half expected him to tear off his humanoid mask, revealing a lizard like set of features. Martin resolved to soften his approach.

"Do your parents know you're here?" He ventured.

This elicited a more measurable degree of panic as evidenced by their expressions.

"Yes, sir." The boy squeaked.

This was clearly a lie but he knew that further pressing the issue wouldn't probably exhume more clarity. He conceded a stalemate was not an entirely undesirable outcome. He didn't need any witnesses to his potential career ending scandal which was tenuously concealed mere feet from their current position.

"You kids run along now. This is an official police matter. If you will kindly remove yourselves from the premises in a timely manner, I will forget I saw you here and won't consider you on our list of possible suspects as far as breaking and entering is concerned."

Martin felt he couldn't've worded that any better and it seemed to be taking the desired effect. The children at first appeared to have uncontentiously accepted defeat and had all but made it past the point from whence they came were it not for the unavoidable gurgling sound, slithering from the crevice beneath the slightly ajar supply closet door.

Now it was Rosicky's turn to elicit anxiety, pitifully stammering in an attempt to obscure the emerging white noise.

"What, wh-....what were you all planning to do here, anyway?"

They didn't seem much in a hurry to leave; he must try to increase their discomfort, thus inviting their voluntary exit. Too many humanizing characteristics and mannerisms had convinced them he might be a somewhat trustworthy figure and they were inclined to answer with a degree of veracity. What is it about the intentions of a being that can be so quickly discerned by children and dogs?

"Sir, no." Maddy was searching for the appropriate combination of nouns and verbs. "It's just the town is gone crazy. I know you know. I can tell."

Martin couldn't've found her clumsy verbage more comforting. "And so you thought you'd go to the one place that might be safe." He tried to help along her thought to manifest. "Where you might find some answers." It seemed they had all too much in common.

"Yes, sir." Patrick picked up the baton. "Sir, please help us. Please don't make us go back out there. It's not safe." Rosicky could hardly contend with the logic.

Maddy intended to lay her hand on the table for all to see. If there was one person in this God forsaken hell hole they could trust, odds were it was the fat, ironic man.

"Sir, we've been through so much. Please help us. We lost our best friend. He was killed by a monster. We don't know who to ask for help. No one will believe us. So we came here, to find Pastor Coleman."

This little bonding session would come to an abrupt closure, though. Whatever was churning in the supply closet now burst into their company. Apparently, Rosicky's missile had failed to deliver a death blow and the creature, high with adrenaline and indignation, had flung open the door and inserted itself into the discussion. It was a mélange of fangs, claws, scales and an other-worldly blood like substance, it's wings spread wide in a tell all of it's majesty. Though it's stature was decidedly wanting, the volume displacement with it's flight regalia in full display was more impressive. This coupled with the deafening screeching ordinance it purveyed, amplified by the generous acoustics the hallway provided, it demanded to be acknowledged. Martin complied with a volley from the maw of his 9mm fire breathing dragon, riddling it's lizard like mass with four additional rounds, effectively dispatching it from this realm beyond speculation.

Patrick and Madison had reposited themselves aback from the snaky antagonist and were already recoiling back to a more tranquil state. *No need to sneak about any more with these guests at least* Martin concluded.

"It was like that." Maddy volunteered from the cover of Patrick's shielding embrace. "But bigger."

Rosicky arched an eye brow pensively. "Bigger?" He felt his heart drop. He now lamented the absence of one of APD's assault rifles. If not, then at least an RPG from Camp Round Horn would do. But this was all an exercise in futility.

"You say there's bigger ones than this that killed your friend?" Rosicky ventured timidly.

"Much bigger." The terror in their eyes told Martin they'd made no exaggeration.

He gulped audibly.

Now an unsettling pair of choices was unfolding before him. Although he was keenly aware of the growing discomfort in the 180 degree exposure at the midpoint of the long corridor, surely, with every moment, the odds of their detection increased and this had him yearning for Pepto-Bismol. But alas, he was not excited about the prospect of pushing forward with the added baggage of two hormonally imbalanced adolescents but the alternatives seemed wholly unsatisfying and cold hearted even.

Rosicky eyed his steads with skepticism. He wanted to tell them to "Scram! Get out of here." So this could all just go away. But would he be virtually sending them to their death? And what if they leaked on his little 'excessive use of force' foray on a Federal Endangered Species Act protected animal and new darling of the scientific community? That was a scenario he was eager to avoid. He fidgeted with the items in his pocket, anxiously looking for some pros. But they did have field experience with these alien animalia and, as they stood before him, unwavering in their conviction, he was admiring their resolve and determination in the face of danger. He would not assuredly be exposing them to dire straits in one form or another but it occurred to him that the difference was nothing more than a coin flip. Maybe they could at least watch his back or something. *Some high priced sulfur mine canaries*, he thought to himself.

"Ok, look." Martin grimaced. "Stay close behind me and don't make any noise. We're going to find Pastor Coleman."

They warily continued their trek deeper into the heart of the religious facility. They stopped after so many meters to examine Coleman's office, though it was clear upon arrival that no one was likely inside. The door had been battered and was hanging partially by one set of hinges, it had clearly seen better days. Closer inspection revealed the insides had been gutted in true rock star fashion. Papers were strewn about, file cabinets violated. Patrick scurried over and checked what would normally be a competently latched closet door which, from careful observation, he knew to house a safe where the offertory collections were stored. Predictably, it too had been adulterated and it's naked insides could be easily discerned by the ajar pad lock covering.

They solemnly coalesced beyond the office and began making their way closer to the narthex. The implication was that the sanctuary was the hub of the wretched happenings, they all seemed to sense this. Now they waddled closer in a crouched stance to avoid potential detection and also because of a detestable stench was beginning to make it's presence felt, meandering to their respective nostrils, announcing it's entrance in a most disagreeable way. They first curled their upper lips, hoping against hope it was only a particularly unfortunate fart but as their distance closed, it only became less palatable and they were forced to shield their olfactory senses with their sleeves, whatever filter they could manage. There was also a smoky aspect to the dreadful atmospheric antagonism they were encountering, causing their eyes to burn and visibility to decrease incrementally, based on the rate of their advance.

The trio ducked low to mitigate the hazy environment, waddling into the narthex the long corridor ultimately spilled out into on high alert. The fire truck red carpeting and regalia, though soiled, was a clear indication of their current location. Adjacent to the majestic wooden doors of pine, the entrance to the sanctuary, a waist level glass pane had been implemented for observation purposes. Here a pesky toddler could be cajoled without disruption while the spectacle of the weekly traditions could still be consumed. They stayed low, virtually crawling up to the portal to sneak a peek at what was taking place in the great hall without squandering the unannounced nature of their infiltration. What they saw when they furtively poked their eyes over the sill, they could never have prepared for and their innocence would be forever altered.

Their attention was first drawn to the deplorable, upside-down crucifixion of one Pastor Barry Coleman, bound taught from three points, the tasteless renovations all but unnoticeable in contrast. Coleman's corpse could be seen to let blood, dripping and splashing below on none other than a hapless, caged Challista Coleman, too traumatized maybe even to know the source of her gruesome shower. She clamored about as best she could, given the claustrophobic confines of her little makeshift pen, in a hysterical manner, mumbling inanities with a wild look seared onto her poor face. It reminded Rosicky of a field mouse recently inflicted by a snake bite, desperately trying to escape an ailment besieging it from inside it's very being.

The foreground was composed of a mob in contention, chief among it's representatives the spear armed imps. A heated debate was ensuing, the central figure of which.....there he is! It was Simon. Martin's eyes bulged with the onset of the revelation. Still clad in the Russell Athletic black hoodie he'd confiscated during his miraculous escape from the asylum.

Despite all the controversy, morale seemed to be high. The mass was red hot with gung-ho! As they peaked their ears to vie for a vantage point with which to gage the dialogue taking place inside, Rosicky had half a mind to shield the youngling's eyes from the grimy debacle. It was wholly inappropriate for the forming mind of a pubescent person to be enduring but the task at hand took precedence over that and he dismissed the urge to do so as quickly as it had arisen, reasoning that their innocence had already been perforated effectively, given what they'd already bore witness to and if they were truly to be of any assistance in the coming saga, they, like him, would require the full value of whatever reconnaissance there was to be gleaned. He was going to have to start viewing them less as wards and more as peers on this sojourn into the heart of madness.

Although the glass observation window was decidedly thick and the imposing pine double doors were effectively sealed, creating a vacuum and allowing for a bit of sound proofing for the ceremonies conducted inside, someone had given the consideration of leaving the P.A. system on, which was actually transmitting the proceedings somewhat clearly to those who found themselves in the lobby. They observed with awe as the spectacle unfolded. Glorduk, the inferred leader of the imps, appeared to be petitioning Simon who, for some twisted rationale, had adopted the name of Freeney. Martin deduced this to have something to do with the implied new found 'liberation' he was experiencing.

"Worshipful master," The lizard like imp, with various horns and tusks jutting indiscriminately from it's scaly flesh, spoke in a ghoulish, raspy cadence like that of Igor/Smeagol of J.R.R. Tolkein lore. "Let us waste not a moment more. We have possession of The Book, The Believer's best weapon. As head of the raiding party what oversaw the procurement of this artifact, I demand that we strike now, in our moment of triumph. Let us utterly destroy this outdated relic and usher in a new era of devastation upon this pitifully frail realm. Our numbers are adequate in order to wage a successful incursion. Let us move out from this position and, unfettered, we might soak the earth with the blood of those insolent bastards who would dare to stand in defiance of the one true power in the universe."

Glorduk had developed a substantial following. His incitation roused a hearty elation from a notably diverse cross section of the wicked congregation. Freeney was quick to reestablish order.

"Fools." He declared.

This garnered suspicion from the audience. They were anticipating Simon's enthusiastic co-sign.

"We shall not move out upon the lands of the sheep." He addressed the throng. "Tempting, though it may be, it is the volition of an imbecile to rush to conclusion and act on emotion."

Glorduk wasn't having it. From afar, one might conclude a mini-mutiny at hand.

"Master!" Glorduk slammed the hilt of his spear against the floor in protest. "How can you now rob us of our decisive victory? This is lunacy! I'll not stand by idly as you revert to a catatonic state of apathy whilst our brethren persist firmly in their resolve on the front lines. As procurer of The Book, I lay rightful claim to it."

He inched forward a talon, gesturing toward The Book that Gary might surrender it without incident. "It should be destroyed. The Praetorian Guard will overse-......"

Glorduk was intercepted by the furious Freeny, eyes bulging with rage beneath the brim of the black hood which was his trademark. He had seized Glorduk's quivering body in a fluid motion and hoisted him over head as though he were a halfway decomposed forrest log. Freeney gave the likeness of a burly man here but taking into consideration the diminutive nature of the imp, probably closer to the 75lb mark, coupled with advantages afforded by the adrenaline rush of anger, along with the element of surprise, Simon could quite feasibly be capable of tossing Glorduk like a rag doll; which is precisely what he proceeded to do, much to the dismay of the astonished onlookers. Apparently, there existed an understood hierarchy, the composition of which seemed to be in the balance.

Glorduk bounced and flopped from the tumult of Freeney's body slam like a trout having been cast onto the ground from some body of water, shock in it's eyes as it gasps for air. Perhaps more than the sheer force of the capsizing event was the symbolic nature of the catharsis. Back in Hell, Glorduk held a position of prestige. But here on Earth, it was a bitter pill to swallow. This was Freeney's show and he had made that undeniably clear to all.

Simon flexed his muscles, eyes burning with scorn and damnation. He was eager to fill the subsequent void with propaganda.

"Let these fool hardy numb skulls rush like lemmings to their demise. If any wish to follow in their misguided efforts, they are free to do so but they do with little effect."

The crowd was once again at his disposal as Glorduk had not made an attempt to recover to a more dignified bipedal stance. He remained prone, licking the wounds of humiliation like a cocker spaniel having been kicked by a grouchy master.

"No. Not today. Only fools rush in at the onset of victory. It is a false promise. We have come too far to make another vain attempt at reconciliation. Yes, the enemy doth rest thine weary head unknowing of the impending danger gathering in these chambers and a modest triumph we may seize but it is merely masturbation for the short sighted. Lest a keen observer go silently in the night, there are far greater ramifications at stake.

"I, Freeney, shall guide us to a new, never before seen level of achievement. You want this realm? This miniscule, pathetic fleck of dust in the wind. You may have it, I say!"

All were fixated by this and unsure of an appropriate response. On one hand, they so desired to be set free to scavenge and scour the land of men as they had fantasized of doing for so many eons but they sensed, correctly, that it was a set up.

"Ultimately," he continued. "In the annals of time it would be remembered as an adorable little foray into enemy territory. A side note.

"No, my friends. We, here, do strive for greatness! I say we take advantage of this windfall and strike directly at the root of the problem......The Crystal City!"

The decrepit army watched in awe as Freeney once again produced The Book with the white tree symbol emblazoned upon, the focal point of all the controversy.

"Instead of destroying this weapon, what if we fully utilize it's nuances to our own constructs? All I need to demonstrate this is the hand of a Believer. Ah, here. Yes, Challista, this will do. I knew there was a good reason to keep you around, aside from the obvious. My, Gramma, what great tits you have. Ah ha ha ha ha ha ha ha!"

This elicited a muffled snort of humor from the audience. Doubtful she was even aware of the proceedings taking place in her vicinity, she gave her hand without resistance when Freeney bent next to her humble cage and borrowed the use of her paw, placing it upon the cover of The Book. No sooner had he done this did the white tree symbol began to glow and shimmer like fairy dust.

The pages flipped open. Within the leaflets it could be seen the individual names of those chosen to be raptured during the end times. They were illuminated with effervescent light from The Book.

An apparition now projected itself of glowing celestial light, no more than three meters above the floor. It was thought there to be a tear in the very fabric of reality itself. A hovering portal had appeared, accompanied by a supernatural drone like intonation. This star gate, whose resolution was superbly clear and mercurial, was depicting, quite visibly, an aerial view of The Crystal City itself, Capital of Heaven! All bearing witness were enamored by the clarity and allure of the phenomenon they were watching unfold. It was such an unexpected turn of events, Rosicky was forced to rub his eyes in disbelief. The angelic, harmonious tone, much like that of a tuning fork, hung in the air, temporarily cleansing the environment one might perceive, sparkles abounding. Martin mused briefly if he was somehow an unknowing participant in the most intricately planned Mr. Clean commercial of all time.

Upon closer observation, one could now see more clearly the details of the majestic, hallowed metropolis in all its glory. The portal also seemed to possess a telescopic capability that would even adjust directly for the auspices of the respective viewer. As the zoom effect began to close in little by little, it was noted that the structural composition of Shangri-La was that of a completely translucent, crystalline substance like that of the most remarkable quartz. The inhabitants of these massive high rises were going about their daily routines seemingly unfettered by the inherent lack of privacy. They adorned beautifully and intricately woven robes of various colors and the nature of the crystalline structure also appeared to possess a technological aspect to it as well, which they casually interacted with, displaying images, mural format, of their various loved ones on Earth in real time.

Now it could be seen that The Great City in the Kingdom of Heaven was dissected by a body of water that was more closer in resemblance to a sea. It, too, was of impeccable clarity, allowing the voyeur to gaze all the way to the depths, miles and miles of the purest water filled with a number of aquatic animals engaged in a perpetual ballet-like stasis. Different crafts, both marine and air, were acting as ferries, shuttling citizens from one side to the other. The picture painted was that of a bustling community, yet infallibly tranquil at once.

Freeney was licking his chops at the innocence on display before him. Even he, with this visionary level of faith in victory, had not imagined a day in which he would be able to peer into the enemy's fortress undetected. The irony was quite profound as he was realizing his dream of seeing God's Kingdom.

"You see?" Simon leveled an index finger at the reflection of The Crystal City. "Only fools rush in. If we attack now and strike at the heart of the enemy's staging point, we will catch them unawares. This planet...." Freeney struggled to find the words. "Is a means to an end. Should we successfully conquer it in it's entirety, there will forever loom the shadow of a great threat to our dominion. But let us push forward, at all costs, right at the belly of the beast and let our oppression be felt where The Believer's arrogantly enjoy their retirement and we may yet separate the head of the snake from it's body. We may, in our time, actually bring an end to the conflict and bring about an era of conformity and decisiveness. Let this day forever be known as our Independence Day, just like our forefathers demonstrated for us but a few centuries ago. Let us fight now and forever secure our FREEDOM!!!"

The crowd combusted into an uproar. They all instantly volunteered to be on the front line, forming a queue at the base of the chancel. Freeney was now hoisting up the goblin like creatures one by one, clutched by the waist as a toddler might be, and loading them into the portal to Heaven head first. As he did so, they unraveled their bat like wings that they might glide and/or parachute, smoothly descending upon The Crystal City from high altitude, the star gate readily absorbing them into the other dimension. Martin and the youngsters watched in horror as the ravenous imps looked to take on a more formidable stature upon touching down onto various high rises, proceeding to wreak havoc and terrorize the wholly unprepared populace. It was a field day for the imps. They moved from dwelling to dwelling, pillaging and plundering, leaving fires and ruination in their wake, virtually unopposed.

CHAPTER 21

"We have to stop them!" Maddy's eyes bulged with fury.

Martin was so disgusted with the proceedings, he dropped his head low as he could feel the bile surfacing, jutting into the back of his throat. But he caught himself on the brink of evacuation, luckily it was nothing more than stomach juices, he'd neglected meal time, and thought better of it. It was an unfortunate disposition but he was tough enough to swallow it back down, along with a remarkable grimace. He did not want to portray weakness right now before his, albeit wanting, precious few allies on either side. He knew he would need every bit of their resilience to confront this situation. His whole life had been building towards this. He knew he was going to die today.

"Hey, Mister. Snap out of it." Patrick was firmly jostling his shoulder. "Someone's coming. Down the hallway."

Martin was catapulted back to his senses. This was no time for a pity party. Verily, he was given no false warning. Someone or something was approaching from the long corridor very quickly as evidenced by an ever nearing battle cry echoing though out the acoustics of the narthex. There was also a substantial amount of radiance being emitted from that which was closing in on them with great speed.

Rosicky's adrenaline finally kicked in, giving his eyes the frantic pace needed to ascertain a quick hiding place for them. Martin did not want to initiate a confrontation without knowing precisely what he was dealing with. Even though it was well concealed and the odds of it's discovery by Detective Martin Rosicky considerably low, especially given the atmospheric conditions, through some act of sheer serendipity, he could, perhaps given the various vantage points of light created by the flickering candles and also the fast approaching nemesis in the hallway, faintly make out the outline of a rift in the panels adjacent to their position in the narthex. Throwing caution to the wind, he lowered his shoulder and bull charged through the neatly hidden secret door. Expecting more resistance (apparently it wasn't even locked), he barreled through into the abyss of some nook, the contents of which made for a rough landing. He was sure he'd broken some items in there and possibly shattered some glass too but there was no time to discern the nature of this. Unwilling to acknowledge the pain he was enduring, he hastily picked himself up and ushered the kids into the cavern with him, shutting the door behind them virtually coinciding with the arrival of the 'whatever it was'.

They found themselves a tangled heap of limbs and nervous, sweaty panting and at the mercy of a rather limiting set of confines. It was dark and dank and they found themselves feeling around like blind cave salamanders on various objects they'd spilled over onto. Shin and ankle were encountering heavy resistance here. Somehow, the kids managed to find enough room to gain solid footing. Martin had not strayed far from the door where he'd recovered to a crouching position. There was actually a fair bit of chasm between the bottom of the hatch and the flooring and he was dutifully inspecting this, trying to monitor the goings on outside in the church foyer. There was just enough room in this crack for him to peer out with one eye, his face pressed against the ground.

No sooner had he done this, than the source of the awful noise and increase in lighting was revealed. It was the pin headed, burning man as described previously. This time, his entire body was aflame brilliantly.

"Aaaaaaaaaaaaaaahhhhhh!"

He had been sustaining an epic battle cry for some time now.

"Aaaaaaaaaaaaaaahhhhhh!" Was the decided exclamation as he burst through the sanctuary doors to join his cohorts in their invasion ploy with the help of a generous running start.

He must've been happy as hell because he didn't seem to have paid any mind to the trio. Martin felt it safe to now ascertain the nature of his current location.

"Somebody turn the lights on." He grunted.

The kids complied with a synchronized effort, feeling up walls and groping about objects indiscriminately. After a procession of clumsy movements, Patrick was the first to strike gold.

"Here it is. I found it."

It was a pull string light bulb in the center of the modest room. Now having been illuminated, it could be seen to be Pastor Coleman's antechamber. A small, discreet room next to the sanctuary where he would, on days of observation, change into various robes and also housing a baptismal font for blessing items such as the communion wafers and wine. Along with this revelation came with it the awareness that they were not alone. The introduction of light had disturbed the hibernation sequence of a stowaway imp having entrenched himself on top of a wardrobe closet and wrapped in his wings neatly like some ghoulish burrito. It was already hissing to life with outrage and spread wide it's wingspan. They hadn't much time to react before it was already air born and tumbling earthbound in an impending swan dive trajectory towards poor Martin.

He didn't have the mental dexterity to assess things, ready his weapon and get off a shot in defense. Only a knee jerk instinct afforded his hands to shoot up and brace for impact.

SKREEEEEEEEEEE

Although these creatures were decidedly modest in size, the element of surprise and the added inertia of gravity was enough to send them both somersaulting onto the floor and subsequently the perimeter of the cozy nook in a convoluted mass of fangs, teeth, claws and fists. Rosicky was sustaining a myriad of scratches and cuts but he was ultimately, most likely due to the disproportionate disparity in weight, able to gain the upper hand. One could see he was angry. He reared back and brought down a blow upon the hapless reptile. This might've rendered any normal man unconscious but the imp appeared to have a noteworthy amount of tenacity. The wicked animal actually was able to recover with great agility, squirm it's way free and leap frog around to Rosicky's shoulders, wrapping it's legs around his neck and began raining down talons upon the detective's scalp. His only defense was to clasp his head with interlocked fingers and hope to absorb the flurry of scales and claws.

His allies finally entered into the equation with Patrick, having neither the where with all nor time to be picky, conveniently snatching up the nearest object with real heft to it, in this case a large ceramic jug of communion wine, and smashing it down upon the rabid imp from behind with velocity. The dynamic devolved into a blur of scarlet colored velvet, communion wine and ceramic fragments discharging in all directions. Perhaps the imp ambusher had completely discounted the presence of the teenagers because the momentum of the crushing utensil, albeit with a generous accumulation of verve, probably wasn't enough to subdue the angry varmint on it's own but it still managed to dislodge the assailant from Rosicky's back, hurling it to the ground.

Then an unanticipated effect began to take place. Rosicky was hobbled over, coughing and choking, trying to regain his bearing from the assault but his attacker was experiencing a considerably less enviable set of circumstances. Apparently, an ingredient contained in the 'Jesus juice' was eliciting a drastic type of allergic reaction from the creature's skin. There was an audible hissing noise illustrating this in a most unavoidable way as steam rushed to escape and squeeze through it's tightly woven scales. The trio watched with astonishment as the imp writhed in pain. The contrast was so dramatic, Patrick was reluctant to rush in and apply any finishing blows for fear of contagion. The beast literally appeared to be melting. It's flesh seared and popped as though it were bacon frying upon a griddle. The imp was now gurgling and foaming at the mouth, a dazed expression glazed over it's snake like eyes. It began emitting a series of distressed screams of agony and incredulity. It was as though it were crying out against it's very flesh, begging it to return to it's normal state as it was cooking before their very eyes. It was a meltdown of epic proportions. The trio was now forced to shield their eyes and nose from a disconcerting amount of gasses produced by the sizzling effect of the chemical combustion taking place. The imp let out a final guttural protest as it surrendered it's life to the communion wine. The whole thing didn't take long for the acid like effect of the wine to consume the majority of the imp's mass leaving behind a sticky, greasy mess. Not much remained; an amalgam of ooze and maybe some singed bone fragments.

"Well, that was unexpected." Came the understated remark from Rosicky as he was recovering from the choking assault. "Hmm, this stuff is pretty good."

His attention now turned to the contents of the antechamber. There were four or five jugs of the potentially tide turning 'Jesus juice'.

"This could be our ticket out of here." He observed. "Only problem is: there may be too many of them to splash at. Maybe if we wait until their numbers dwindle down, a few well-placed wine grenades can cripple them and I can finish off what's left."

"But that would mean that so many of them would've gotten through to Heaven." Maddy pointed out, her voice quivering with grief.

It was an unsatisfying supposition, he was forced to agree. Martin stroked his moustache pensively.

"We need a delivery method. Something…"

The trio fell silent with deep thought. It was an anxious, final jeopardy style interlude. Every increment of time passing, as Madison had keenly identified, meant more troops infiltrated into the heart of The Crystal City, bypassing the security measures and reveling in a free for all, Golden Corral style, 'all you can eat buffet' of mindless self-indulgence as it were.

"Wait, I've got it!" Patrick sprung to life with a brilliant epiphany. "Hold on."

"Wait, don't go!"

Martin desperately tried to stop the boy from bursting out of the antechamber trap door and back into the church lobby but the young man was on a mission he was clearly devoted to. He disappeared into the grimy environment, leaving his comrades to wallow in the suspense. They hadn't been particularly moved to blindly follow him into the unknown, especially with all those hostiles lurking about and Rosicky, although he was tempted to, didn't see the upside of potentially sacrificing the unit behind the ill-advised whims of a teenage boy, no less.

Although it may have felt like eons, Patrick didn't keep them waiting long. He returned back to their cubby hole with arms full of…….arms. Only, more appropriate weaponry for children it seemed.

"I forgot all about these." He confessed.

Pastor Coleman had a small stockpile he'd

confiscated and stored there in his office closet, Patrick recalled, subsequently following a church pot luck in which it was deemed by Mrs. Simpson that the squirt guns too closely resembled the actual gun violence all too prevalent in the modern news cycle. The general consensus among the presiding adult supervision was in agreement of this assessment and Patrick had silently lamented this but never forgotten their location, where they had stayed for lack of impetus for the greater part of three months.

Now the Super Soaker 250's, virtually brand new, glistened and gleamed in all their splendor, seemed more like a master stroke if only Coleman were endowed with such clairvoyance but none the less, here they were and boy, did they look good!

Patrick had made studious choices from the selection at hand. The 90's relics had come fully equipped with camel back style reservoir drums allowing for considerable ammunition holds. Along with the modest, plastic bubbles contained upon the sizable assault rifle squirt guns, each unit might be able to hold roughly a gallon and a half! There were two squirt gun assault rifles Patrick had procured but not knowing their efficacy for anything other than the imp nemesis' they prepared to face, Rosicky thought it best to outfit the kids with these. They would probably know how to operate them better anyway and he simply felt more comfortable with the stopping power of the trusty 9mm in his possession, though with no more than one or two clips at his disposal. A co-ordinated strike would be pivotal to their success.

Morale had been given a dramatic boost. There was even a hint of a smile in their eyes as they took turns pouring the ceramic jugs of communion wine into their respective auxiliary drums of the Super Soaker 250's and proceeding to strap them on and test the contraptions. With a fair amount of pumping the squirt guns, as is necessary to generate the pressure needed to pro-pel the fluid magazines they were privy to, it was deemed their range to be not all that bad. It was a firm stream, Martin estimated to be able to con-sistently reach a distance of 10 yrds with a meas-urable degree of accuracy. Things were looking up for the battle tested, rag tag unit of volunteers.

Rosicky readied his troops: "OK, so the main thing we have here is the element of surprise. Once we leave out from this closet, there's no turning back. You guys, I want you to flank me on either side. Wait for my command to open fire, we may need to conserve ammo."

He tried not to view them as minors in this instance. They were his best bet and actually well qualified, all things considered. He whispered a tiny prayer to himself and closed his eyes for a sol-emn moment, asking God for strength for what he was about to do.

Dr. Kovac paced back and forth methodically.

He'd developed a syncopation to the rhythm of his steps, hands clasped behind him like a Carpathian count, to match the progression of the cuckoo clock and the ever unquenchable 'drinking bird'.

Tick – Step – Drop

Tock – Step – Drip

It was as an unwavering perpetual motion machine.

"What is the location of the detective at this present time?" Came the transmission.

"They've reached the target destination. Everything is going according to plan." Dr. Kovac answered so calmly and in an uneventful tonality as he winced slightly, staring out, blankly, into the courtyard of the sanitarium facility.

The image of what they spoke was displaying on the surface of a sizable crystal ball, a volleyball sized object resting alone on the center of Kovac's mahogany desk. Slightly skewed to the curvature of the spherical device, Rosicky could be seen discussing with his youthful entourage from their present location of Pastor Coleman's antechamber adjacent to the mighty Abundant Grace sanctuary chamber.

"Give an update when it is done." Came the final transmission.

Kovac did not feel obligated to respond. He smoothly about faced and glided over to Mr. Hudgens, seated in the middle of the office with his head canted backwards. He casually pressed a small, furtively placed, flesh colored button behind Hudgins' right ear. Following suit, the constructs of the cyborg's skull began locking in place much like a Rubik's cube, concealing the sophisticated communication apparatus in Mr. Hudgins' head. The form of a human was restored and a normal conscious look returned to his assistant's eyes.

"Thank you, Mr. Hudgens." Dr. Kovac nonchalantly stated.

They then resumed a spirited discussion concerning the Green Bay Packers.

CHAPTER 22

The great cherry wood doors of Abundant Grace sanctuary hemorrhaged out Detective Martin Rosicky. On either side of him were a boy and a girl, no more than 14 or 15, replete with squirt gun rifles and sizeable auxiliary ammo tanks slung onto their backs.

Brandishing his 9mm service pistol, he announced their presence thusly: "Gary Simon, stop what you're doing! I'm here to return you to custody."

The grim army, nearly half depleted by this point, had been caught unawares and they strained to reconstitute themselves towards the unwelcome disruption. Freeney had been wearing a look of glee as he was euphorically loading imps one by one into the floating portal to Heaven. This expression waterfalled into a grimace of disdain as the realization of their intrusion fully saturated.

He dropped whatever imp he'd had in his arms as though it were a murder weapon and he'd been caught red handed. Leveling an accusatory finger, shaking with fury at the heroic trio, "Outsiders!" He emoted. "Seize them!"

The morbid mob reacted in kind. Though their volume had been focused at the front of the worship area where they'd been clamoring for position to perpetrate their daring assault, the setup of the pews caused them to be essentially bottle necked there. Some imps, frustrated by this, began desperately catapulting themselves over the top of the pews, trying to spread themselves out.

The closest enemies to the trio were the sex crazed soccer mom's at the end of the invasion column. It was none other than Mrs. Bethany Simpson, having taken up the caboose position in the raiding party, who showed no hesitation. She rose up, clad in a provocative garter belt and panties ensemble and let out a hideous hissing noise of contempt, much like that of an alley cat, and motioned toward them with awful intent.

Rosicky did discharge the Glock (the silencer attachment had since been removed) into her sternum, leveling her instantly.

BLOW!

Her hapless body plopped to the floor most ungraciously. She let out a series of guttural, bear-like groans as she arched her back, somehow trying to escape the pain of the hollow tip round, fragmented though out her abdomen.

The dark mass stopped in it's tracks, stunned at the turn of events. The gall of these people to shed the blood of his majesty's army! One could hear a pin drop.

Freeney exhorted them, "Kill them!" He yells, spittle spraying with rage.

The hellacious squadron took to a Blitz Krieg style attack. It reminded Rosicky of some twisted Alamo reenactment. As the enraged acolytes of evil descended upon their position, Rosicky bided his time, waiting for the most precise, calculated moment.

"Now!" He commanded the children. "Unload!"

Patrick and Maddy wasted no time unleashing the devastating effects of the communion wine ordinance. They calibrated the concentrated streams of purple, snaking back and forth from side to side, touching all points of the first wave of aggressors as they approached. It could be seen that not much of the consecrated substance was needed to render undeniable stopping power as the 'Jesus juice' instantly began eating their scaly flesh upon impact.

A substantial number of their party was virtually eviscerated. The psi and range of the Super Soaker 250's had allowed this. Essentially half of their strike force were now writhing in pain, if not fully disintegrating altogether into a disgusting ooze. This so terrified the remaining attackers, many of them felt compelled to hastily abandon the battle field. Some that stayed, simply ducked for cover wherever they could manage and were devolving into hysteria. Freeney's attack squad was all but compromised.

Now, with Freeney's red sea of footmen having been parted, the trio was free to approach the worship area virtually unfettered. Freeney reluctantly back peddled, matching their consistent advance lockstep.

Things were a little bit different now. The tables were turned with Simon's evil mob disbursed. Half having been released upon The Crystal City with a mission of chaos and reckless abandon, the other half having been utterly neutralized by the merciless downpour of Jesus juice from the well-armed youngsters under the command of one Senior Detective Martin Rosicky.

"My babies!" Simon lamented as he regressed towards the majestic pipe organ which scaled the back wall of the chamber, reaching towards the stain glass display.

"They're not your babies, Simon!" Rosicky taunted. His nozzle trained on the rogue escapee. "You're confused. The devil doesn't love you! Come back to reality. Let's go home. And maybe one day you can have some babies of your own."

"You fool!" He shot back. His grim look turned quickly to a flash of defiance. "Will you not realize until it is too late?"

As calculated, the question was allowed to linger, causing Martin's slow march to adjust.

"This is bigger than life." Freeney was obliged to expand. "Eternity is a long time, you pig. You wish to spend it in bondage?"

"The servitude is with your master, Gary, and you know that! I'm not buying what you're selling."

"You believe everything you're told, don't you? You petulant little child!" Freeney countered. "You've been taught to think that way, so that it might be easier to harvest your souls whenever your greedy, selfish creator so desires. Ha! You can slave your entire pathetic life, only to be rewarded with eons of more whip cracking from your "all loving" father."

He was met with silence this time. Either Rosicky was tuning him out or his words were planting seeds of doubt within him. Freeney was eager to rush in and fill the gap with more propaganda.

"Don't you understand the struggle of the oppressed? Yearning, striving, reaching for any kind of chance at freedom. It's ok, Martin. Admit it, everything you've ever been told is a lie. It is a rigorous and unwavering system of control. You are not treated with respect. You are but a gerbil in a cage, running ceaselessly in you little spinning wheel, never reaching your potential. Nothing more than a docile little pet."

"Shut the fuck up!" Escaped from Martin's chest. Freeney had been really pouring it on and Martin was cracking.

He could feel his hand fighting his index finger's urge to squeeze the trigger and end it. Though the pressure from his pointer finger grew, he was deliberately not allowing the hammer to be activated. Something was keeping him from doing what he felt in his heart to be best. Perhaps he wanted to hear Gary out. Difficult sometimes to eradicate a mindset one does not understand.

One good reason not to blow this bastard's head off, he told himself. *He's opened a portal to hell for God's sake. What if there are more?* He envisioned the use of a Patriot Act inspired water boarding. If ever there was a just time to employ this tactic, would it not surely be now?

A sliver of practicality urged Rosicky to abandon the likelihood of taking him into custody alive. Would be more satisfying, he reasoned, for the perp to spend eons behind bars, ultimately even forced, maybe, to confront his own warped outlook. Of course, he'd already escaped once before. And his principle's certainly were firmly cemented by now. *This man is more dangerous than Hitler*, he thought.

But if one could go back in time and assassinate a would be tyrant before his rise to stardom, should they not? But that would be too easy and it was already past the point of having any real preventative impact. *Just once*, he told himself, *I'd like to see one of these maniacs pay for what they did.* Besides, if Simon dies then would he not receive what he actually wants? A reunification with an evil overlord pleased with the good faith of his loyal servant. He would ascend to rock star status in the halls of Hades.

He resolved to continue his gradual lessoning

of distance between them before he could tackle that asshole. It'd been some time since he had to physically subdue a perp but the adrenaline was telling him that it would be a welcome development.

Freeney had now run out of room to back pedal but he could sense Martin's dilemma. Blood in the water.

"Why?" Freeney continued. "So you can drown out valid reasoning when it is presented to you?"

His expression changed. He appeared to be in deep thought. Something was being conjured in his mind. He closed his eyes, visualizing some mental download. Oddly, he seemed to be processing a moment of commiseration.

This clearly emboldened further the Luciferian. "Don't be a fool, detective." An unabashed look spreading across his face, "I've seen your solitary, lonely life. We're all friends here. I know how you can't be open about your temptations, curiosity of the finer things in life. I know all too well the Lord is an unreceptive audience to the needs of men."

Simon shifted his stance and adjusted his groin to reveal a standing erection bulge, more resembling the anatomy of a pachyderm, Martin was forced to visualize. His shock and appall was enough to stop him in his tracks.

"That's right, Martin." He was now somehow aware of his name. "I know of your deepest, darkest fantasies, pony boy."

With each word, he tilted his hips and let his arms dangle halfcocked in a display of effeminate poses. Martin felt like an injured bird under the abuse of a particularly cruel tabby cat.

"We can rule this realm together, with me as your lover, and all the wealth and riches He never saw fit to share with you. For my master is a most generous one; he can," Gary broached the subject more tactfully, "even restore the health of your poor mother's lungs and eliminate those pesky tumors in her chest. You're God just hasn't seemed to be able to find the time." He tossed in a forced expression of empathy and then leveled a punctuating jab. "Mine will."

This struck deeply to Martin's core. He yearned to realize the wonderful things Simon spoke of and he toyed with the idea of their actualization. Perhaps his firmly rooted cynicism would be his saving grace. A lifetime of disappointment fueled his skepticism. If he did give admission to his desires and made an agreement with the devil's associate, what would keep that deal from souring by some unspoken variable? He recalled the plight of so many figures in history. Surely those who'd been given the misfortune of attracting the scope of his investigatory mechanisms could be counted as the result of some of these same exchanges and he knew all too well the unenviable position they ultimately arrived to. Rosicky thrust himself from his deluge, hence: he did not like the effect this escapee was having on him or his cohorts. He did not like what him and his allies had done to his town. And he could not justify placing his good faith in their ways.

"No!" He shot back. "Those are hollow promises. Restore my mother's health you may do and fulfill the whims of my heart you might but there will be some trickery there in. You offer me a perversion of satisfaction. In Jesus' name, I rebuke you!" Saliva sprayed with damnation.

Freeney recoiled in indignation at Rosicky's rebuff, the steadfast dedication to ideology perhaps the most abhorrent quality of his foe. He winced at the prospect of what he might be forced to do. There was disappointment too. The determination of a loyal clergy member or hopeless disciple was to be expected but he was convinced that the psyche of a career law man was supple fodder for corruption. They'd witnessed firsthand the brutal and unforgiving nature of the world, not to mention the dehumanizing, desensitizing perversions of mankind. The work was renowned for a complete identity subversion, the case most ideal for demonic interference.

Martin was now bearing down upon his target. Simon was cowering before his tormentor, minimized in the shadow of the grandiose pipe organ. The senior detective could reach out and grab him if he wanted to but thought better of it. There's no telling what tricks he might have up his loose fitting sleeve. He could sense Maddy hugging tightly to an escort pattern on his left. There was relief in that the kids had shown great prescience by following his lead and not opening fire on their own accord, though the temptation had surely been there.

Simon is just a man, he mused. *He may know a few spells but they are just that.* By the same token, the 'Jesus juice' cannon also was not presumed to be considered an equalizer in regards to mortal flesh.

Detective Martin Rosicky reared back his hand to strike. His intention was to cold cock Gary, ideally rendering him unconscious but he was thwarted yet again with a plea from Freeney.

He wore an expression of an otherwise healthy puppy being offered up on the chopping block by some heartless farmer. The flash of vulnerability might've been the only thing that saved him were it not coupled with an outburst.

"I'm taking you in, Simon."

Gary abruptly shrunk back into a ball and made an incantation.

"Alabaster, protect me!"

Martin instantly felt foolish at his naïve yen for contrition but there was no chance at self-chastisement given as the giant, cannibalized, stained glass mural depicting the Messiah exploded into shrapnel, raining debris in the form of countless shards upon the altar area caused by none other than the hulking gargoyle bearing the name 'Alabaster', plummeted to Earth in the form of an onyx egg, it's gargantuan wings wrapped around it into a sort of spring roll of terror. This revelation was hidden from the trio until they could remove their arms from their brow, the naturally ready-made, instinctive shield. Alabaster's entrance demanded their attention, the behemoth shaking the very foundation of the edifice with his landing. He must've weighed at least 500lbs.

Rosicky was quickest to take action, primarily motivated by unquantifiable fear, discharging the clip in it's entirety in the direction of the beast at close range into it's upper torso region, more closely resembling an abyss of fangs and muscle. The slugs were promptly enveloped as though they had never existed. Alabaster rebuffed into a proud stance. The rounds had lodged into it's thick, pelt-like skin, surely causing some degree of discomfort but no significant damage. It was akin to shooting a buffalo with a pellet gun. It stood there with it's hands on it's hips, flexing in defiance and emitting a bellowing, maniacal laugh.

"He, he, he, ha, ha, ha, ha, haaa!"

Martin was frozen with terror. Alabaster effortlessly swatted him aside like a gnat, sending the full grown man flying from the altar area, contorting into a heap, the front row of pews the final destination of his landing point.

Maddy had no time to lament. She drew up her weapon and nudged the nozzle in Alabaster's direction, letting fly with a compressed stream of communion wine concoction his way. Alabaster reflexedly rewrapped himself in his wings creating the spring roll of darkness defense shield. The 'Jesus juice' barrage pummeled his outer layer, gas emitting from the point of impact, hissing and rising up. She continued to let loose the super soaker until the stream strength waned for lack of pressure.

There was quite a bit of mist formed. When Alabaster eventually moved, retracting the voluminous wings, it was revealed that he had been completely unscathed underneath the fleshy fortress having been constructed on cue. Freeney found this to be exceedingly amusing. Laughing uncontrollably, he wasted no time to mock what remained of his captive audience.

"You fools! Only now, as it is too late, do you see the folly of your futile ways. The Great Culling is inevitable."

Freeney added an exclamation point in the form of a rigid back hand to Madison's hapless face which resulted in her dismissal from the standing position she had so recently occupied.

Alabaster continued to revel with his domineering pose of pride. His fists on his hips, towering over the decimated scene, it was almost as though he had become the new idol in this tawdry display of vandalism and carnage.

This may have proven to be all too much for young Patrick, who's presence was announced now. In the preluding chaos, he'd managed to shift his way over to the pulpit area. No one had deemed fit to stop him. No one had noticed. There was too much going on. But now he found himself in the true position of power. Amidst all the boasting, the posturing, the jockeying for position, the great debate, the turmoil, he was now in possession of The Book, it was foolishly unguarded. For an adolescent, he was remarkably intuitive. A natural leader, his gut always seemed to direct him, seemingly against the grain, to those outlier sweet spots that proved time and again to either make or break in those pivotal moments. Some describe it as a voice inside, coercing them to make adjustments not routinely considered by most, in an anything but routine world. Though at times it seems our spirits yearn for predictability, for others it is more of a subtle prompt and for some even, an undeniable urge for that leap of faith which defies logic yet proves as the catalyst in so many historic moments. Custer's Last Stand, The Battle of Gettysburg, The Battle of the Alamo. It was at this moment and at this point in the timeline that Patrick did seize The Book.

Some ethereal mechanism then took over his motor skills. A bright, golden aura was activating from his upper torso. This snapped his posture, violently arching his back, thrusting one arm to the side, whilst the other maintained The Book held out. It fluttered open but seemed to leave his control. The luminescent phenomenon then built with intensity until it reached a critical mass, concentrating at his solar plexus into a blinding orb. The orb proceeded to blast a concentrated beam into The Book which took on an equally charging effect. Patrick appeared to be floating now with kinetic energy.

A grimace befell Simon. "What madness is this?" He conceded. "He has The Book! Somebody, stop him!"

But his footman ranks were woefully depleted. Alabaster was truthfully the only one who could've realistically answered the call for help but he seemed to be profoundly disturbed by the supernatural occurrence concerning The Book. He was visibly unsettled, his nostrils flared with indignation. He hadn't exactly leaped to fulfill his master's commands either, it could be noted.

Gary looked on with horror as the energy beam coalescing in The Book discharged dramatically into the very depths of Alabaster. He was rendered immobile from the blast, a vain attempt to shield himself with his forearm. The beam flowed steadily into the creature for what seemed like a great deal of time.

Then it finally ceased.

There was no more aura to be seen from The Book or Patrick who complicitly collapsed from the exhausting emittance.

Alabaster, the great hulk, was in much worse condition. He was struggling immensely from some vengeful form of dysentery, he appeared to be bubbling from within. His expression twisted and contorted, finally, and it had the look of ex-cruciating pain, he threw his arms out, concerning his back, arched rigidly. A mercurial, blinding light was seeping through the crevices of his hyde-like flesh, which favored as though it were harden-ing. And rapidly at that. The skin crackled and split sporadically. Now every orifice on his face was overcome with the vociferous, uncontain-able light. It was undeniably consuming him from within.

Alabaster let out a last roar of despair before he was overwhelmed by an inescapable burst of light which convoluted the large sanctuary cham-ber in it's entirety. All that remained of poor Ala-baster was a neatly composed pile of sooty ashes.

Freeney was distraught with emotion. "No, my beautiful gargoyle!" He lamented. Stooping over, he grasped a handful of blackened remains.

Jumping up to his feet, wringing his hands at a nonexistent audience, "There will be hellacious torment to pay for this!" He was gritting his teeth with rage. "I will spare no expense, give no quar-ter. The kingdom of Heaven will be brought to it's knees with --------- ach!"

His diatribe was cut short from the severed iron beam having impaled him through his lower back. It was none other than Challista on the other end, twisting the rod to slump Simon's paralyzed carcass to the ground.

"You ruined my family, you bastard!" She pro-claimed with righteous fury. "Aaaaaaahhhhhh!"

She began screaming hysterically. It was all too much for her psyche to withstand. She collapsed into a traumatized, sobbing, wide eyed ball there and began sucking her thumb like an infant.

The scene relaxed now as a motionless period was allowed to permeate through the cavernous hall, the only sound, a celestial tonality emanating from the still open portal to the Crystal City. There was a various assortment of body parts, corpses, muck and grime, ash and soot, smoke and sticky haze. It was deplorable.

Ultimately, some movement.

Challista remained in her child like state, whimpering and muttering to herself indecipherables. Maddy was the most apt, perhaps the only one of the trio having not been incapacitated in one shape or form.

She rushed quickly to his aid. He was already stirring.

"O, Patrick." She caressed his face. He was eerily calm. Like a mother who had just given birth, serene in her contribution. He simply shot back a playful smile.

"Where's Martin?"

Her expression turned to concern.

"I don't know. He took a hard fall." She furtively glanced over her shoulder. "Come on, let's get him."

Patrick effortlessly popped up. They hurried over to the disheveled heap that was Detective Martin Rosicky. He was lying face down, unconscious but still breathing.

It took the two of them using all their strength to flop him over. He was not a slender fellow.

"What do we do?" Madison gasped.

The unspoken prospect of being the only ones alert enough to answer for all of this a real factor. Of course, it wasn't their fault but who would believe them? Whatever they said.

"Slap him." Patrick suggested.

Maddy's eyes replied with incredulity.

"Seriously?"

But it wasn't such a far-fetched solution. Never mind that Patrick himself had not offered to do so.

"Can we do that?"

Which was a silly response. They'd already broken so many laws and unquestioned boundaries thus far. But it aptly demonstrated their innocence.

Patrick nodded in approval.

Madison summoned the courage to do what surmounted as a pat on Martin's cheek.

"Harder." Patrick whispered.

WAP

But Maddy grew tired of the games.

WAP

WAP

But it was finally enough to rouse Martin from his involuntary slumber.

"What?"

Martin reluctantly returned to this plane.

"It's ok." She consoled him. "The monster's dead. Patrick killed it."

Martin's eyes bulged with the severity of the update.

"Simon! Where is he?"

A dedicated dog catcher, his first concussion induced coherent phrases concerned his culprit.

He hopped up like a rake having been stepped on by accident but it wasn't long before he could deduce that there would be no need for a post custody interview.

"God damnit!" He slammed his fist into a cupped hand, secretly relieved that there would be no threat to the world from one Gary Simon. But this was one asshole he really wanted to see suffer and rot away in a dungeon somewhere.

Challista killed him, the kids thought but didn't say. They understood the adult need for paperwork and also the injustices of it that may follow.

"We need a blanket or something." It was a matriarch that had seen her entire family slaughtered before her very eyes in a most gruesome and insidious way.

The gentleman Rosicky took off his beige, now tarnished, trench coat and draped it over her but she was not looking to be disturbed. She leapt up with terror and urgency. Howling, screaming, she thrust off the trench coat. Stark naked, she bolted out of the sanctuary with deceptive velocity.

The trio was reluctant to follow after her. There was no guarantee as to what was outside of the church and she was not to be reasoned with. Though pity they felt, it was for the longevity of this Earth to which their hearts turned.

It was a new day. Along with it, unsettling and disturbing questions. The worm had turned. The rules had changed. All the tales were true. They wished they could somehow capture this series of events in a mason jar and seal it from the imagination of man. Sequester it from the collective mind.

Rosicky retrieved his nice trench coat from the floor. It was then that he was reminded of the police frequency walky-talky in the breast pocket. It wasn't on but he knew they would be coming. And he did not want to answer any questions. He did not want to deal with his peers. He did not, in any way, want to be associated with this grotesque and sickening occurrence.

"We should set fire to this place." He muttered. "And never speak of it again."

This didn't sit well with the kids.

"But the portal to Heaven, it's still open." Maddy chimed. "What if more of those things get in there? Then nothing will matter."

Martin regarded this with mixed emotions. Was he really having this conversation with a 14 year old?

But it was difficult to argue. The scenery was

still fresh and the point was more than valid. There literally was a portal to Heaven open and hovering before them. The implications of this were staggering.

As a group, they crept over to the pulpit where the portal lay some feet above. The Crystal City could be seen shimmering and gleaming in all it's glory. They could even make out the sparsely scattered imps harassing it's citizens in a frenzied and desperate way. Surely they were overwhelmed with the experience having never prepared for a day when those walls would have been breached. They would probably be corralled eventually. But after what amount of destruction.

"We *have* to stop them!" She proclaimed.

The kids looked to Martin for reaction but he was bemused and lacking of a concrete response, flummoxed.

"Patrick," the debate moved to the two young ambassadors of Earth. "It's up to us."

Patrick, the more cerebral of the two, considered this. But serendipity had more to contribute. Some poor footing on Rosicky's part, the stumbling over the latent corpse of an unfortunate imp, caused a slight collision with the podium where it was revealed that there was a hidden stow away compartment located inside. An out of place looking wooden panel, not affixed by any competent means, was jostled loose allowing for the encounter of yet another interdimensional portal. How long had that been there? Nobody knew. But it was decidedly different in nature.

This thing took on the attributes of a sinister red glow and a much lower vibrational tonality. The animalistic instincts endowed to us could communicate effectively the evil what lied there in.

"Look, there's another one." Patrick indicated. Though it's presence had not escaped any of their awareness.

Upon closer observation, it could be determined that this was in stark contrast to the Crystal City apparition. Here we have the portal to Hell. And it was quickly deduced that this was most likely the mysterious introductory point of the ghastly imp creatures.

Martin had been reduced to a strictly observational role, an unwilling captive of the proceedings. Perhaps internally he had conceded on some level that his ultimate mission was the apprehension of Simon and anything beyond that was no more than speculation and quite arguably unnecessary. He was vastly out of his element. So much for training. There was just no protocol for Biblical disaster containment and the events he'd endured found him musing about retirement on some tropical island getaway, exotic drink in hand. He didn't want to stay. He didn't want to leave. He wanted to pull the covers over his head and make it all go away.

But it was not going away.

He even flirted with the idea of using all his

expertise in tracking down individuals intent on evading detection and cashing in his chips as far as his public life was concerned. He could, for lack of a better phrase, flip the script and use all of the techniques he'd gleaned from the very fugitives he'd hunted for years to change identities entirely and become a veritable ghost, existing solely off of the grid and neatly under the radar. He could wash his hands clean of this ridiculous, macabre charade. Besides, he'd done enough, saving the world and all. Is that ok?

Martin looked on helplessly as the kids unilaterally came to a conclusion about what was to be done next. Another jug of the 'Jesus juice' was hastily retrieved from the antechamber and administered into the Super Soaker 250's auxiliary reservoirs.

Patrick looked young Maddy square in the eyes and gaged her, "Are you sure you want to do this?"

"Yes, Patrick." She shot back firmly. "What choice do we really have?"

The question lingered in the air.

"Our friends are gone." She continued. "This town will never be the same again. We.....will never be the same again. The police are looking for us. And I don't trust them. And my father!" She exhaled in defeat. "I don't even want to know."

Patrick weighed this carefully. Then Maddy pressed on.

"But even if we could pick up the pieces, Patrick, it wouldn't matter. Someone else will have to go through this again. There will be another Freeney. Our town might be safe for now but what if this happens somewhere else? We were lucky!"

She capped off her thesis with a firmly placed jab to Patrick's chest, driving the point home. It was a terribly astute thing to say. Most girls her age would be clamoring eagerly to a return home and the comfort and warmth of their beds. Perhaps her angle was somewhat influenced by the prospect of being greeted with her dad's iron clad rule and the idea of making a clean break altogether had entered her mind on more than one occasion in the past, as some young people are prone to ruminate.

The couple's eyes met in a heartfelt gaze, "Do it for Rory." She uttered.

And this carried the desired effect. Witnessing the horrific death of their dear friend who'd sacrificed his very life for them had thoroughly robbed them of their innocence. And they knew it. It was a climactic moment in their evolution.

Patrick gently, calmly, reached out and grasped Maddy by the shoulders with nothing more than his fingertips and delivered a priceless, once in a lifetime kiss to his story book crush.

When their moment finally subsided, they were looking at the floor, a little embarrassed perhaps or self-consciously aware. They took a deep breath, ventured another glimpse into each other's eyes, then descended into the portal to

Hell.

"Well, that was brave." Rosicky mused quaintly.

Two otherwise normal teenagers had just willingly entered into the gates of hell in hopes of saving the world, armed with nothing more than communion wine enhanced Super Soakers.

Maybe it was good, their innocence, their naiveté. Anyone more practical would not have made that decision. But by that same logic, perhaps yet they were the only ones suitable for the job. That which exposes them to great danger is also that which protects them from it.

Rosicky considered all this as he drew in the environment with his mind's eye. Sparks crackled from the Bible bonfire still smoldering in the corner.

No. This was no world he wished to inhabit any longer.

Martin made another glance around the room to make sure no one was watching. He retrieved the flask of Wild Turkey 101 from inside the breast pocket of his trench coat and gulped down a generous apportionment. Then, he reloaded his 9mm service pistol, took a deep breath and heaved himself off of the podium and into the portal to Heaven.

The End